TWO WORLDS

On that day, men of all nations thirsting for power and greed ignited the World by the touch of a button. The Earth was left barren and almost void. For years' darkness was on the face of the Earth.

Story by
BILLY MARTIN

authorHOUSE®

AuthorHouse™
1663 Liberty Drive
Bloomington, IN 47403
www.authorhouse.com
Phone: 1 (800) 839-8640

Published by AuthorHouse 07/08/2017

ISBN: 978-1-5246-9618-4 (sc)
ISBN: 978-1-5246-9617-7 (e)

TWO WORLDS

In the midst of the waters lay the iron relics of another age, broken and rusted. The dryland was scorched by the power of the flames and the surface was littered with ash, and the wreckage of man's creation was scattered by the power and the force of the blasts.

The Earth that brought forth grass and fruits trees of all kinds now took the shape of skeletons, bent, twisted and blackened.

The light that ruled the day was scarcely visible and the light that ruled the night was never seen, only talked about. The once blue sky was now a canopy of gray and black clouds, clinging together like coral around the Earth.

Every living creature and every living thing that moved according to its kind was sprinkled throughout the land.

But man survived and walked the Earth through the wreckage of his own destruction. Cities which once stood tall and proud, now stood as a beacon of the past, a shadow, housing the legacy of mankind and his abilities to create from the old World.

Caleb Cantu, like others, survived through the blistering furnace. He traveled through the remains of the old World toward the West Coast in an effort to reach his only living relative, his father. His journey is met by others who survived, but now survive for different reasons. Those who search for the meaning of life, and those who wish to rule by power, greed, and force. This is the story of those Two Worlds as they collide with each other.

CHAPTER 1

Life underground takes a little time to get used to. Not seeing the sun for 4 years leaves you a little pale and skid dish. Amid all the inhabitants that made their way to the underground shelters in time were those who had paid attention to the what was going on and were close enough to the underground shelters before the blasts started pounded the Earth. Caleb Cantu was one of those. Once a journalist for a local magazine, he maintained a steady relationship with the news media and the local government officials. His message tried to prepare his readers, but panic has a way of forcing people to do just the opposite.

Caleb was 33, single and the athletic type, and takes good care of himself. He lived in a high-rise apartment complex in the Mid-City area. A building that was designed with lots of glass windows. Featured as one the Cities most desirable buildings. He knew that when life was about to be eliminated by the World powers, staying in a glass building was the last place one would want to be at. Caleb wanted to survive. He made it to the underground shelters as the first of the blasts occurred, and there he remained for the entire event. A long 4 years. But now it was time to come out of the Earth to the surface. The officials were instructing those who were ready to gather their personal things and make their way to the Central Departure Door. The announcements stated that the air outside was acceptable for living. There was no longer a threat of radiation. Each person would be given a supply of water and several days of food rations before they departed.

Caleb gathered his personal items from a cardboard box he kept under his cot. The bunkers he lived in was crowded with others who had made it in on time. The entire facility held close to 2500 people, all crammed together in concrete rooms. It was safe and designed well and protected those who were fortunate to make in. Singles were placed in one area and families were designated to another area. The military maintained law and order along with the remaining local police.

The facility was designed with living quarters and feeding areas and was stocked with dry goods and water. An underground system of tunnels allowed the officials to move about, keeping and maintaining communications with other units. Medical staff, organizations that provided educational training, and other needed agencies were designated into each underground unit.

Caleb carried his bag to the Central Departure Center and provided the guard his ID. It would take several minutes before he would be able to leave and he would need to be checked one last time. He would receive instruction on the conditions outside and a stiff warning about those on the outside who survived, and the danger that would be present on the surface.

"Mr. Cantu would you step this way." A man's voice

instructed him. He was a tall man wearing a military uniform. A man of some rank which Caleb didn't recognize.

Caleb followed him into a small concrete room where several others were standing and waiting. Most he didn't recognize but he knew they had been underground waiting for their chance to return to the surface for whatever reason.

"Mr. Cantu it is my understanding that you wish to leave this facility and go to the surface? He asked. "We want you to know that once you leave there is no returning. We must protect those who remain here from disease of all types. I'm not saying that there is disease out there, but if there is, we cannot have it here amongst this population. Do you understand and agree to that?

Caleb dropped his items to the floor. "I understand and agree to those conditions." He replied as the others listened and watched as he signed the forms. He stepped back and picked up his items.

"Each of you will be given a back pack if you so desire." The solder stated. "You might want to use them rather than carry boxes."

Caleb took a backpack and repacked his items and then adjusted the backpack to fit his shape. It was heavy but at least his arms were free. They were escorted to another room where several doctors and nurses gave each of them shots and some pills to keep on them. They were instructed to the importance of the pills and when to use them. Caleb listened carefully and placed them inside his pack. Another solder led them down a long hallway to a metal door. You could hear the mechanical devices working as the metal door began to open. They were led through the door into another room. The door closed behind them and suddenly a fog filled the air.

"Don't be alarmed" a voice said, "This is for your protection as well as ours. Once the fog clears the door in front of you will open to the outside. You will have only minutes to exit the room before the door closes. We wish you all the luck, there is the New World."

Suddenly the door began to open. It was a thick door and the air from the outside began to filter into the room along with some dim sunlight. The air felt thick and had a strange smell to it. As Caleb entered the World he stopped and looked around. The door began to close. The buildings that once were a beacon of man's creative design were nothing more than rubble. Very few remained and the skeletons of others stood twisted and bend to the ground. The skin of the buildings laid piled in heaps, battered by the weather. Vehicles of all types were blackened and rusted from the explosions with only their frames remaining. Caleb looked into the sky. The clouds remained heaped together like cotton balls, black and still. Rays of sunlight passed through cracks in the clouds providing some light. The ground was dry and ash rose from his shoes as he started to walk. The others who were with him walked slowly as well taking in the sight of the Earths remains and the City they once knew.

Every corner, and every street was the same. Destroyed with only small ruminants remaining. He could hear something or someone echoing along the buildings hollow walls. Some building still had their names on the sides. Scared, and blackened, you could still read some of the letters. At each intersection, the stop lights were nothing more than melted metal and metal poles were bent in half almost touching the ground. As far as you could see, building after building were destroyed. Their insides gone, not a table or chair remained. Caleb thought about those that stayed behind when the blasts began. He remembers the ground shook like an earthquake for days. The sound was deafening and the heat from the blast was be on anything a person could possible endure. He remembered the children inside the shelters crying as the earth took note of the blasts, rocking and shaking to a point that one could not stand up.

Caleb needed to find his bearings. Which way is West? Not being able to see the sun made it difficult to distinguish north from south. He continued walking in the direction he thought was west. West is where he wanted to go. His father was in the West, San Francisco. He had tried to contact him prior to the big event, but phone lines must have been down. His father was the last of his family. His sister and all his family died in the early blasts destroying her building. Nothing remained but the concrete base and a few pillars.

As he rounded the corner he recognized the remains of a small building. Its walls stood upright, and the red sign partially remained above its double doors. The old Woolworth Building. He now knew he was traveling in the right direction.

"What I would give for a cold soda." He said as he passed by the remains.

The street was filled with debris, scorched vehicles and shattered building. Everything laid amid the buildings. Some vehicles were stacked one on top of the other.

As he reached the end of the street he saw what appeared

to be a grayish cloud coming his way. It stood tall and appeared to be moving quickly toward him

"Ash clouds," he thought. "I need to get to cover."

He had heard stories of clouds of ash being blown in like rain smothering everything in sight. He quickly ran inside a stripped building. He looked around and saw what was left of a storage room. Its door was still in tack. He opened the door and was hit in the face with something that knocked him to the ground.

"Get out, this is my space. Find your own." A young voice stated as the door slammed shut.

Caleb shook his head and got up from the floor. He was covered in ash. He wiped his face clearing his eyes. He saw the clouds getting closer and decided to make another advance on the storage room. This time he would be prepared for whatever was in there. He opened the door again and again an arm through a punch this time missing Caleb. Caleb grabbed the arm and through a punch of his own. It was a solid and whoever was there is now down for the count. He quickly jumped inside just as the wind storm reached the building and the thick clouds of ash started filter inside the room as the door slammed shut.

"Say, what's the big idea? The young voice stated as he raised up.

"There's an ash storm out there and I didn't have a place to go, but this will do." Caleb replied. "Who are you and what's the big idea hitting me?

"Everyone must take care of themselves, that's what." The young boy replied as he wiped his lip. Blood trickled down the side of his jaw. "Man that hurts."

"If it was anyone else, they'd be in here and you would

be out there so, this is your lucky day." Caleb said. As he placed a rag over his mouth. Although the door was solid and a good fit, the fine powdery ash still found it way in through any crack of the door. "Here put this over your face," as he handed the young boy a rag. Don't worry about a little blood. You're lucky your head is still on your shoulders."

CHAPTER 2

"What are you doing here? Caleb asked.

"What are you doing here? The boy returned.

"Alright, let's start over again. My name is Caleb Cantu. Where is your family?

"You're walking on my family. They were killed and turned to ash just like everyone else around here."

"You mean you're by yourself? How do you live? He asked

"You sure ask a lot of questions mister. Where did you come from? Not from the surface. You must be one of those underground people I've heard about."

"What underground people? Caleb asked.

"There's a story going around that the underground people are just now starting to surface. There's large presents of military searching for street people who are robbing those from the underground, mostly for their food and medical items. Are you one of those underground people?"

"Yeah, I'm one of those underground people." Caleb replied.

"You got anything I can eat? The young boy asked.

"Yeah, I've got some things. Are you hungry? Caleb asked.

"Are you kidding, I could eat a horse, unfortunately there all gone as well." The boy said.

"Where did they go?

"Into a large pot somewhere."

Caleb reached into his backpack and pulled out a small package of dry good items.

"If I'm going to share this with you, you can at least tell me your name? Caleb asked.

"My name is Robert. Robert C. Washington. I am a direct decedent of the first president of the United States, George Washington."

Caleb looked up at the boy. "Here take this Mr. President, it will take a lot of chewing, but when mixed with some water it will expand and keep you full the biggest part of the day. Here is some water."

The young boy took the items and devoured the dried food and drank the water quickly. He held out the cup wanting more. Caleb poured a small amount. "I need to use this cautiously. I'm not sure where to get more water."

"The underground water is controlled by the military. It's hard to get there and they're very tight amount giving it out. But I can show you where it's at. You were right, when you drink the water you swell up. What is this stuff? The boy asked.

"I'm not sure." Caleb replied. "But you're not going to die from eating it."

"Where are you going? The young boy asked.

"I'm heading west. To the West coast, California."

"California? On foot, you're going to go to California?

"Yep, that's where my father is at." Caleb remarked as

he repacked his backpack. "That's where he's at and that's where I'm going."

"Well, I'm going with you."

"What, who says you're going with me?

"I did." The boy replied.

"Well, maybe I have something to say about that."

"What are you going to say? I live on the street. I know how to handle everything on the street. You've been underground so long you lost your touch. You don't know anything. At least with me you've got a better chance."

Caleb thought for several minutes and then turned to the boy. "Okay, but you take orders from me. I don't want to be responsible for your death if things get out of hand."

"If things get out of hand it will probably be me helping you. You need to understand the World is no longer what it used to be. Survival is the most important thing." Robert explained.

"Let me check out what's going on outside." Caleb replied as he slowly opened the door, peering out and then opened it further.

"Looks like the ash clouds are gone for now. Let's get a move on Mr. President. We need to find shelter before the night closes in on us. What's that like? Caleb asked.

"Dark." Robert replied. "Very dark."

They exited the building as the ash still floated in the surrounding air and then slowly covered the ground and everything above it. They walked several blocks until they reached a street sign that was laying on the ground. Caleb brushed off the remaining ashes and stood up.

"Look at that. The sign says West 10. What luck?" Caleb remarked.

"That sign could have been somewhere else and just landed here. We need to have real directions. Come on I know a place nearby that should give us the right directions."

They walked for several more blocks until they reached the remains of what was a large building.

"Come on, in here." Robert directed. "Over here."

"What is this place? Caleb asked.

"It's what's left of the train station for this area. Over here is a board with directions. It's still standing. Look there. West 10. You were right. That's the right direction. "Suddenly they heard voices coming from inside the building. Robert grabbed Caleb's arm and pulled him behind a pile of rubble that was once the ticket counter.

Two men enter the building. They were dressed in ragged clothing but carried weapons strapped to their back. They walked through the building looking in all direction, then turned back around and left the way they came in. Robert and Caleb watched as the two men left, still huddling behind the counter.

"I think their gone now." Robert stated.

"Who were they?

"Those are the bad guys. There looking for anyone who came from the underground. We need to be careful. The closer we get to the outside of the City the more careful we'll need to be. See I told you you'd need me. If I wasn't here, you would be wanting to share your items with them and chit chat with them. Then when that was over they'd take your stuff, then shoot you."

Caleb looked at Robert the President and agreed, he better spend more time learning what he can from this boy.

"I think we better spend the night here tonight and try for

the city limits at first light. I think we'll have a better chance of getting out of town in the early morning." Robert stated.

They agreed and found a more suitable location to spend the night in the existing building. Above the counter area was a stair case that led to the second floor. Most of the stairs steps were missing and that would make it more undesirable for others.

"No fire," Robert stated. "Unless you want the entire remaining City here with us tonight."

Caleb thought to himself. "This kid is full of everything. How do you know so much? He asked as he prepared a bed roll.

"I've been on the streets for several years. So, I've learned how to survive, where to go and where not to go. Who to talk to and who not to talk to.

"Where's your bed roll.

"I don't have one. They took it from me.

"You haven't got one, so you can share this with me and who took it from you?

"The bad guys."

"Men like those we just saw?

"Men just like them. There all over the City and especially at the City limits."

"Why the City limits? Caleb asked.

"The crossing into the country is where people try to go to get out of the city."

"Is there other places we can go to cross without having to go there? Caleb asked.

"Yeah, but it could be dangerous. The terrain is every difficult to get across and many have died trying."

"Well I don't plan on dying so let's give it a try." Caleb stated. "You'll led the way Mr. President. Good night."

CHAPTER 3

The night came and went without incident. The morning was cold and the smell inside the building was musty and thick with wet ash. As Caleb moved about he quickly noticed that Robert was gone.

"Just what I needed, the most knowledgeable person has now abandon me." Caleb remarked.

He rolled up his bed roll, packed his backpack and slowly made his way down the stair case to the main floor. He was careful not to make any noise. When he reached the main entrance to the building he was stopped by Robert.

"Where you going." Robert asked.

"I thought you left."

"I got up to see what was going on outside. If we're going to try to reach the rocky area and get across, I needed to know what we're up against." Robert replied.

"And?

"And what? Robert replied.

"What are we up against?

"Nothing, it's clear all the way there. Let's go."

The two journeyed through the remaining city ruins to an area where Robert had said would lead them out of the city and avoid the crossing at the city limits. It took several hours to reach that point and both had to stop and rest.

"We need to eat something." Caleb stated as he reached into his backpack and pulled out the package of dry goods that was given to him.

Each took a small piece and each drank a small portion of water. After resting they continued walking past the last of the ruins. At the edge of what used to be the city limits, they both viewed what was in front of them.

The thick forest was no longer there. What remained was the remnants of a different forest. Standing as twisted and blackened skeletons almost ghostly in appearance. Just be on the edge of the trees one could see the rising mountains that bore no color. The green grasses were gone and the rocks were now pebbles of different shapes and sizes.

"Look there." Caleb pointed.

Robert looked in that direction and saw one lonely tree that had new foliage growing. New leaves appeared on its lower branches. Its upper branches were scorched and broken is several places.

"Looks like life is returning." Caleb stated. "Come on let's go."

They moved through the blackened forest until they reached the base of the mountains.

"Climbing up this mountain isn't going to be easy."

"What's on the other side of the mountain is worth it. We'll avoid the problems of the bad guys and we will be able to join up to the main road that will take us West." Robert remarked as he started to make his way up the mountain. Caleb followed closely behind him.

The climb was difficult. Many of the rocks were small

and loose which made finding solid footing a major concern. If you slipped and fell it would be serious. The larger boulders had sharp edges and made it difficult to grab hold of. After several hours, they reached mid-way. Exhausted from the climb, they rested. Suddenly they heard something in the distance. Caleb looked up and saw what appeared to be a light in the sky coming in their direction.

"What's that? Caleb asked

Robert jumped and shouted. "Come on we need to find some cover." As they both hurried off. Robert led them to a gap in the boulders big enough for two to stay hidden. They each wedged their bodies into the crevasse and remained still.

"Okay, now that I'm stuck in these rocks, what's going on? Is that the military? Caleb asked.

"No, that's the bad guys." Robert replied as the helicopter came closer until it passed over the top of them. It was a small black craft with two men inside. It hovered over certain areas then moved on to different locations and did the same every few hundred feet until it was out of sight.

"We need to stay here for a while to make sure it doesn't come back." Robert said.

"They roam most of this land, but this is the first time I've seen them over the mountains. I think they know there are those from the underground out and about."

Caleb removed his backpack and wet a small rag and wiped his hands. He had small cuts from the rocks and some were bleeding.

"How far do we have to go? He asked.

"On the other side of the mountain there is a trail that will lead us to the main highway. It's not patrolled as much but we still need to be careful." Robert replied, as he took the rag from Caleb and wiped his hands. "We'll take a different route. One the bad guys don't know about."

"Where's the military? Why aren't they out here taking care of the bad guys as you call them?

"There's only limited resources here, most are located in highly populated areas." Robert stated.

"How do you know so much?

"I've been on the streets for a long time. I see and listen to what's going on." Robert replied as he stood up and looked over the area. "I think we can go now.

They walked for several hours until they reached the upper mountain. Robert pointed to a path that led them half way down the mountain. The heavy charred growth of trees and scattered ash was thick and provided them with some cover from the view of others. Half way down they stopped.

"This is where we're going to change direction. This path will take us the rest of the way down the mountain, but the bad guys know this path as well and they could be there waiting for whoever comes down. I know another way; one they don't know. It's a little longer but I think it's safer."

"Let's do it. I don't need any more excitement today." Caleb stated.

The sky grew darker as the sunlight was denied to shine through the thickness of the clouds. There was the smell of rain in the air and they could feel the moisture in the air against their face. The rain was good, but it was also bad as it thickened the ash like a gray mud and made it difficult to walk through.

"We need to find some shelter. They weather is getting bad."

"I know a place we can go. It's just a half mile or so away." Robert stated as they sped up the pace.

They could move faster as the ground was more solid and free from loose rocks. In a short time, they reached the heavy thicket of fallen trees. Caleb followed Robert around the area until they reached what appeared to be an enclosure made of downed logs and branches.

"This way, the opening is over here." Robert shouted as Caleb moved in that direction.

They enter through the back side just as small drops of rain began to fall. The small rain drops would hit the ash and make clouds of dust that lifted into the air. As they enter inside they were stopped by a barrel of a gun.

"Stop right their mister." A voice shouted. "This is my place, who said you and this runt could enter my place? I should blow your head off for trespassing."

"Wait a minute mister? Robert stated. "This isn't your place it belongs to whoever needs it. Beside you didn't build it."

"Who are you anyway? The old man asked.

"I'm Caleb Cantu and this is President Robert."

"What are you talking about President Robert? This rat isn't no President."

"Look, were moving down the mountain and it started to rain and Robert knew of this place and we just want to get out of the rain. How about putting that gun down, there's been enough death in this world already?" Caleb stated.

"Okay but there better not be any funny business or I will blow you apart." The old man stated as he lowered the rifle down and returned to his seat.

"Here boy, toss some of those logs over there on the fire to keep it going. Since you're here be useful will you."

Robert picked up some of the few logs that were stacked by the opening and tossed them on the small fire.

"So what are you doing here? Caleb asked as he found a place to sit among the junk that was stacked inside the enclosure.

"What am I doing here, what are you two doing here? He asked. "This is my place."

"This isn't your place? Robert replied. "It's been here for a long time."

"Yeah, and how do you know that? He asked

"Because I lead old man Jennings up here and this is where he stayed. He built this place. So, what happened to him? Robert asked.

"Wait a minute, tell us who you are? Caleb asked

"Alright, don't get pushy. My name is Enoch. Last names don't matter so don't ask."

"This is Robert and I'm Caleb."

"Good to meet you Mr. President. I always wanted to have some words with the President. I got some real issues to talk to him about."

"That's real funny." Robert replied.

"So what are you doing here? Caleb asked.

"If you must know, I came up this way to get over the mountains to avoid any trouble from the Black Knights."

"Black Knights, who are they? Caleb asked.

"Those are the bad guys. They call themselves the Black Knights." Robert replied.

"When I finally made it up here I needed to rest and move on the next day. I found this place." The old man who was in here was dead. So, I buried him and remained here since. Some of the rocks gave way and I injured my ankle so I needed the time for it to heal."

"Have there been others up this way? Caleb asked.

"Every now and then someone will venture up the mountains but they never stay. They always seem to be in a big hurry,"

"Do the Black Knights come up here? Caleb asked

"The helicopters fly by one or twice a week but that's about it. It's a lot of work climbing up and down this mountain so they limit their movement on foot. But you can bet you'll find them at the bottom waiting." Enoch replied. "Say you got anything to eat? I haven't been trapping in several days."

Caleb reached into his bag and pulled out the package of dry good items he was given in the shelter and handed both Robert and Enoch some.

"Your one of them underground people? Enoch asked.

"Yeah, I'm one of the underground people." Caleb remarked as he chewed and chewed.

"What is this stuff? Enoch asked. "My teeth aren't that sharp."

"Don't know. Drink a little water and you'll be full for a week." Robert replied.

"Say boy, sorry, Mr. President, what are you doing out here? You an underground person too?

"No. I live on the streets."

"What do you mean you live on the streets? How did you survive and what happened to your parents?

"My mother and father where killed during the blast. We lived in a building that got destroyed and we were trying to reach one of the shelters when another blast occurred. We just made it inside when the blast tore the door of the shelter off and my mother and father were killed. Another family took me in and cared for me. But they were taken away by the military because they were sick. I think it was the radiation."

"You were okay? Caleb asked.

"I went deeper into the shelter where they had sealed off the other areas, I just made it in." Robert explained. "I stayed there for a long time. Then about 6 months ago, I got no calendar so I guess it was about that time, several men wanted out so I went out with them."

"What happened to them? Caleb asked.

"They were captured by the Black Knights and taken away. That was the last I saw of them."

"What's your story? Enoch asked as he continued to chew.

"I just came out of the shelter and I'm heading for the West Coast to locate my father."

"West coast, what city?

"San Francisco."

"And you're going to walk all the way there? Enoch asked.

"Unless you know of another way to get there? Caleb replied.

"Tell you what, take me with you and I think I can find us a way to travel a little faster."

"Me too, I want to go to." Robert remarked as he raised his hand. "I got you this far."

Caleb looked at Robert with compassion in his eyes. And Robert was right, he did get them this far. But the old man was a concern. He must be in his 60's, thin, and wild looking with rags to match.

"Can you walk? Caleb asked.

"If it's going to get me out of here I will fly if needed." Enoch replied. "Fly with a little help."

CHAPTER 4

The rain fell as a mist for several hours and soaked the ash that carpeted the ground. The three slept quietly undisturbed. The air was chilly and the fire provided very little heat. Morning appeared as Enoch was rebuilding the fire. The others stirred as Enoch gathered his belongings and packed them in a bag. When Caleb and Robert finally opened their eyes, Enoch was standing in the center with his bag.

"You guys going to sleep all day? Let's get going." He remarked gesturing to the opening.

"Alright, alright, give me a minute to figure out what I'm doing." Caleb remarked as he raised up from the old blanket that covered him and hard ground he was laying on.

"Come Mr. President the day is wasting away." Enoch said as he walked through the opening to the outside. "You seem to know what you're doing so lead us."

Robert lifted himself up, and wiped his eyes, I need some water." He remarked.

"Over there in the bucket is water." Enoch replied as he pointed to the small wooden bucket.

"Is it any good to drink? Robert asked.

"It's rain water that I gathered. It's clean enough for

drinking. You might want to fill up some containers before we leave."

Robert and Caleb each took an empty container and filled up their own bottles with what was in the bucket.

"Which way are we going? Enoch asked.

"We need to stay along the side of the mountain until we reach those two cliffs that are pointed. The way down will be easier.

"I like easy." Enoch stated as he waited for the two to finish.

They followed Robert as they moved along the side of the mountain. The footing was easier as the shoulder of the mountain had less loose rocks. Within two hours they had reached the pointed cliffs. They stopped and rested before continuing. The packs were heavy and their legs got tired.

"Let me see what up ahead." Robert said as he moved to the lower ridge and then looked the terrain.

"I don't see anyone moving around. But come here and look at this."

"What are we looking at? Caleb asked as he too looked over the small ridge.

"There, over there." Robert pointed.

"Boy, what are you pointing at? Enoch asked.

"Can you see those small boulders, there?" He pointed again.

"The best way to see is to go down there. It's on our way down." Caleb remarked.

They moved down the remaining mountain side and reached the boulders that Robert was pointing to. There amid the boulders hidden toward the back was a pile of items, rags, boxes and a variety of other items.

"What is this place? Enoch asked.

"I think someone was living here, or something. The items laying around look like items you would see in a home. Don't touch anything until we figure out what happened." Caleb remarked.

"I don't think we need to figure out too much, look over here."

Robert and Caleb joined Enoch toward the back and there amongst the piles of rags were three skeletons.

"I think these three must have been living here for some time. I wonder what happened. Enoch replied as he moved some of the debris around so they could get a better look.

"It looks like two adults and one smaller person, maybe a child. The remains are all decomposed the same way." Caleb remarked.

"They died at the same time maybe." Enoch remarked. "Look at the one skull. There's a hole big enough to stick your finger into."

"They were shot. Look at the others." Caleb said as he pointed to the other remains."

"Black Knights I bet." Robert remarked. "Found them here and robbed them, then shot them."

"There's a shovel over there, lets at least bury them." Caleb said as he picked up the shovel and walked to a clearing and started digging a wide hole. The soil was soft from the rain and the hole he dug was big enough for all three skeletons.

When they finished, they gathered their backpacks and continued. The walk was much easier and the landscape was changing. No loose rocks or boulders, but idols of what used to be. Giant trees that once covered the land with their beauty of green and gold, were now barren and black. But time has a way of healing and the further they journeyed the more they spotted new growth.

"Over to our right side is the main highway west. We've passed the outer limits." Robert stated. "But further up ahead of us I haven't a clue what there. This is the farthest I ever been. We need to pay attention to who's around us now."

"If we're going to follow the highway, then I got a special surprise for us all. That's providing its still there. It will probably take us another day or two to get there." Enoch stated. "I sure hope it's still there, I'm not a fan of walking. My feet are flat, and I'm just too old to make these long walks."

"You can stay here if you want? Robert stated.

"No that's okay. I can make it Mr. President. Say, what president are you supposed to be related to? He asked.

"The big guy."

"Who's the big guy? Enoch asked.

"George."

"George who"

"George Washington."

"George Washington, you got to be kidding me. Are you telling me your last name is Washington?

"Yep"

"Let's go." Enoch stated as he walked off shaking his head mumbling something as he moved along.

Hours had past as they were now entering the flat lands. As they journeyed they saw the devastation of the land. Its barren scorched soils were nothing more than dust and ash. Buildings that once stood upright where nothing more than a pile of rubble. Along the walk were signs of a new birth of life as small shrubs were starting to rise from the soil with their green buds begging for sunlight and moisture. Old relics of twisted metal frames stood motionless, rusted and robbed of their identity.

In the distance, they heard a vehicle approaching. They remained off the main road so that no one would see them.

"I hear something coming. Over here." Caleb shouted. "We can stay hidden and out of the way."

They hurried and hid behind the remains of a truck frame. It was burned and rusted without any material other than the metal that held it together.

"Who is it? Robert asked

"Don't know." Caleb replied. "Stay down. Let it pass."

As the vehicle got closer they could see that it was an old truck of some kind. Old with mismatched colors gave the appearance it had been pieced together. Its engine sputtered and rattled as it came closer and black smoke bellowed out from the back. As it got closer to them it started to slow down and then came to a stop. The driver jumped out and opened the engine hood and climbed on the fender.

"What's he doing? Robert whispered.

"I think he's having engine problems. The way it sounds it should have. What a piece of junk." Enoch stated.

The driver was an older man. Hard to tell his age as grubby as he looked. His gray hair was long and in a ponytail with a large stove top hat that was topped off with feathers. His clothes were of many different eras. A mismatch of colors and styles.

"I think we should investigate this guy; he might be okay." Enoch stated. "Besides we could use the truck."

"He could be or he could be something else." Caleb replied.

"We need to take a change on this one." Enoch stated.

"Okay, let's give a shot, but only one of us go. The others stay hidden just in case." Caleb instructed.

"Good, I'll go." Enoch said as he moved out from behind the framework and started walking toward the vehicle.

"Hey there need some help? Enoch shouted out.

"The old man jumped off the truck and reached into his cab and pulled out a rifle and pointed at Enoch. "Who's there?"

"Put the gun down, I'm not the enemy. You need some help?

"Who are you and what are you doing out here? The old man asked still pointing the rifle at Enoch.

"Just trying to get across country to California."

"California, that's a long way to go Mister."

"Well, there isn't an abundance of vehicles to purchase or buses, so walking is about what's left." Enoch stated as he came closer. "You need some help? I used to be a mechanic in the day."

The old man lowered his rifle. "Well if that's all your doing. But don't do anything funny, I'm a good shot. I could use someone who knows something about engines. This old bucket of bolts I found against a building. It was about the only thing that didn't get blown to bits."

"Let me look and see." Enoch replied as he climbed onto the fender and looked inside the engine. He tinkered around with the wires and looked at a few other parts.

"Spark plug wires are bad, but I think I can fix the one that's causing all the problems right now."

He reached into his pocket and pulled out a small knife and began working on one of the wires. After several minutes, he replaced the wire and climbed down.

"Go ahead. Start this thing up."

The old man climbed back into the cab and started the engine. It rattled and smoked but continued to run.

"Well look at that," The old man said, as he shut the engine off. "Do you need a ride? You can ride along with me if you want. My name is Andrew; they call me Andy."

"I could sure use the ride, but I got one special need that really important." Enoch stated. "Well, there's three of us total. We're all going to California. Come out and meet Andy." Enoch shouted as he turned and waved to the others.

Caleb and Robert came out and began walking toward the others. The old man grabbed his rifle and started to point it at the two.

"Put the gun down." Enoch stated as he grabbed the end of the barrel and pushed it down.

"Who are these people?

"There with me." Enoch replied

"Why didn't they show themselves?

"Because you got a gun." He stated as Robert and Caleb arrived. "I want you to meet Caleb and this kid is President Robert. This here is Andy. He's offered us a ride."

"Boy, many thanks. We've been walking for a long time. And a ride is just about the best thing that's happened to us." Caleb remarked.

"Well, okay, but just as far as I'm going. California is not where I'm headed, but you can ride in the back."

Caleb and Robert climbed into the back as Enoch sat inside with Andy. The truck fired up and a cloud of black filled the air as its engine rattled and clanked its way along the highway.

CHAPTER 5

They moved along at a slow speed with smoke filling the air as they winded their way around junk that rested on the highway. The view from the back was filled with emotions as they saw more than what they thought had happened. Portions of farm houses remained standing with only a few reminders of what used to be. Vehicles and farm equipment stood stripped and barren. There tires torn apart and baked from the heat.

"Where are you going? Enoch asked as he watched the truck pull off the main road onto a graveled driveway.

"They used to be a well somewhere in this area. I used to stop here years ago to get water." Andy remarked. As the truck moved along the driveway clouds of dust, ash, and black exhaust filled the air behind the truck. The truck finally came to rest at the base of the rolling foothills.

'I think this is the place." Andy stated as he shut off the engine and got out of the truck looking over the landscaping.

"Where are we? Robert asked, as he jumped down from the back of the truck.

"Looking for some water," Enoch replied as he came around to the backside of the truck. "He says their might be water around here."

"Spread out. If I remember there was a well somewhere around here. It used to be covered by a small wooden shack but it probably has fallen down or gone by now."

Each person went in different directions slowly looking for any evidence of a well. One could see in all directions. The land was as barren as the rest of the land they had passed. Old rusted relics of farm equipment rested quietly.

"Over here, this way." Robert shouted waving his hand to the others. "Over here behind this junky metal thing."

They all hurried and stopped short at what they saw. There, huddled behind the twist metal frame was a woman and a child. Their arms were wrapped around each other and she held a piece of iron in her hand. She was ragged and scared. A child of 6 or 7 was wrapped around her waist frightened. She held a large piece of iron in her hand ready to defend herself and her child.

"Stay back, stay back," She shouted out in a voice that meant business. "Don't come near us."

"Lady, what are you doing out here? Caleb asked. "Are you all alone?

"Stay back." She shouted again.

Enoch stepped forward. "Listen to me, you don't have to fear us, we're not here to harm you, we're just looking for some water. Put the weapon down."

The women slowly lowered her hand then dropped the metal piece she was holding. "Who are you and what do you want? She asked.

"We're travelers heading for the West Coast in that truck you probably heard. We just need some water and we thought there might be some here somewhere." Caleb explained.

"You're going to the West? She asked.

"Yes, that's right. To California." Caleb replied.

"Takes us with you. Please sir, takes us with you." She cried out.

"Calm yourself down, you can go with us. But first is there any water here? He asked.

"Yes, over by the metal pile, there is a large metal plate. Remove it and you'll find some water." She stated.

Enoch and Andy walked over to the pile of scrape metal, found the plate and removed it.

"It's here," he shouted out. "Bring your containers here and fill them."

Caleb walked over to the women and child and stood next to them.

"What are you doing out here all alone? Is there anyone with you? He asked.

"My husband died several days ago. I buried him. We were trying to find his family. They had a farm out this way, but everything is gone. He got sick and we couldn't do anything to help him. He died several days later."

"Okay, you're safe with us now. Have you eaten at all? He asked.

"No, not for a couple of days." She replied.

"We'll take care of that, let's get you some food." He replied.

Enoch filled the containers with water and placed them on the bed of the truck. He walked over and joined Caleb and the rest of the group who stood around the women.

"Why don't we stay here tonight and move on in the morning. We're off the main road so no one can see us." Caleb stated."

"Good," Andy replied. "We can let the truck cool itself down. The engine gets a little over heated at times."

"We need to find some food soon. What I have left isn't much. Any ideas on that? Caleb asked as he gave the women and her child each a piece of dry good from his back pack.

"Is there any game out here at all? Enoch asked.

"There is some ground animals around." The women stated.

"What kind of ground animals? Andy asked.

"I don't know, but they come to get water at night." She replied.

"Game, meat." Enoch shouted out. "Come on Mr. President you're about to learn the art of hunting wild game."

"I've never done anything like this before." Robert stated.

"Don't worry, I'm the best trapper there is." Enoch replied as he walked off with Robert following behind.

"What's your name? Caleb asked.

'My name is Mary and this is my son Simon."

"We're sorry about your husband. This is no place for you, especially alone." Caleb stated as he poured them some water into two tin cups. You can stay with us at least for the time we're traveling. Know anyone in the west?

"No, but it's got to be better than this." Mary remarked.

Enoch and Robert walked the surrounding area looking for any kind of tracks. The loose dirt and ash made it easy to track animals.

"Got the rope and that crate from the truck? "He asked

"Got it right here." Robert answered.

Enoch stopped and then squatted down. "Come over here and look at this. Your about to get your first lesson in tracking signs. See this, those are tracks from a Rabbit. See the size of those prints. The small ones in the front and the larger ones in the back. Let's set the trap right here."

Robert watched as Enoch prepared the trap using the small crate and the rope.

"Now pay attention will you. See how this is done." Enoch stated.

"What's the bait? They're not going to just walk in here?

"What's the one thing that is most needed? He asked

"Water I guess."

"You're smarter than I thought, Mr. President. Pour some water into this cup and place it in the back of the trap. They will smell that a mile away."

Robert placed the cup in the back of the trap and both moved away to where they couldn't be seen.

"I sure hope this works, I'm really hungry." Robert remarked.

Andy gathered some dried branches and other wood items he could find to start a fire. The wooden shack that covered the well had fallen and was scattered in the area. He picked up what was left over and started a small fire for warmth

"We have enough wood to last the night but that's about it." Andy remarked as he found himself a place to sit close to the fire."

"As long as it gives us some warmth and keeps the wild animals away." Caleb stated. "Has there been any wild animals about at night?

"There was a pack of wild dogs that came by just before my husband died, but that was about it." Mary stated.

"We have Andy and Enoch's rifles." Caleb remarked.

"Well, only if you're going to beat them with the rifle. I don't have any bullets." Andy stated.

Caleb gave him a questionable look. "You don't have any bullets for that rile?

"No sir, not a one. Haven't had any for, let me see, a good 3 years I guess." He replied.

"So, if we get into any trouble, the rifle is not going to help us?

"No, but they don't know that." Andy stated back.

Suddenly Robert ran in all excited. "You should see what we caught. Three rabbits, and the last one I did it by myself."

Enoch walked in carrying three rabbits by their ears. "Anyone for rabbit tonight? He stated.

"Come on Mr. President, I'm going to show you how to prepare rabbit."

"I don't think I can handle that. You can do it." He replied as he moved closer to the fire.

"No, you caught it, you need to help prepare it, let's go." Enoch stated as he moved away from the group to clean and prepare the night's fest for cooking. Robert followed behind him still discussing the issue of cleaning.

The group sat quietly around the fire. The night sky was dark and the burning fire provided a soothing touch for the tired group.

"What did you come from? Andy asked.

"We lived in the country about six miles out of town. We had a small farm. Our basement was secure when things started happening. When everything was destroyed, we made our way to see if his parents were still alive. They were the closest family we had. We walked until we reached what was left of their home. When we saw that it had been destroyed we decided to continue hoping to find some people. This is where we stopped. He got sick and died."

"Okay we got as much meat off those rabbits as we could to cook." Enoch stated.

"Where's Robert? Caleb asked.

"He's still gagging from the cleaning process. I don't think he's got the stomach for that part." Enoch replied as he prepared the meat for cooking.

The aroma of the meat cooking above the open flame filled the air. It didn't take long for the meat to cook before the sound of howling could be heard in the distance.

"Seems everyone can smell the rabbit cooking." Andy stated.

"They wouldn't come in, here will they? Mary asked.

"If we keep the fire burning they should stay away, but we need to stay on our guard. We need to take turns tonight. I'll take the first watch." Caleb stated.

"What are you thinking about? Andy asked Enoch.

"I remember being out this far many years ago. I had a part time job stacking boxes and different supplies for the military. I just can't remember where I did it."

Robert walked in and found a place to sit. "I don't think I can eat after that."

"Sure you can." Enoch replied. "It's mighty tasty rabbet."

CHAPTER 6

The night passed by and morning had arrived with the sound of coyotes in the distance. Enoch was the first to rise and wondered about to see what was stirring in the land ahead of them. Andy poured some water and washed his face and began to comb his dangling gray hair.

"What do you think? He asked Enoch.

"About?

"My hair."

"What about it?

"At my age I still have a good amount of hair don't you think?

"You may have a lot of hair but I don't think you'll find anyone to impress, not out here. Now in the city you might find someone who likes your thick white hair, but they'll have to get by the smell first. We need to find a large body of water to bathe."

"Bathe?

"Yeah, bathe."

"In water?

"No in ash stupid, of course in water. When was the last time you took a bath?

"I don't remember." Andy replied.

They gathered their items and loaded them into the back of the truck. Mary and her son Simon sat in the front with Andy as they pulled away. Those in the back covered their faces as the truck kicked up clouds of dust and ash until it reached the main road.

They traveled at a moderate speed slowing down at times to wind through debris that remained on the pavement. They watched for other vehicles but they were alone for the time being.

"Why are we slowing down? Enoch asked as they raise up to see what was in front of them. There standing in the middle of the road was a man. He was waving his arms and shouting something no one could understand. Andy slowed down then stopped. Caleb jumped down from the back and hurried to the front. Andy handed Caleb his rifle.

"Thanks brothers," The man said. "The Lord will always provide in desperate times. And this is a desperate time."

"Who are you? Caleb asked

"I'm the Reverend Forrest P Huckleberry the 3rd."

"Where's the other two? Enoch shouted out.

"Now that's funny my brother. I'm hoping you'll help me out and give a man of the cloth a ride?

"Where you going? Andy asked.

"Where you going? The man asked.

"We're going west." Andy replied.

"Now isn't that funny, that's where I'm going. Can you help a man of the cloth a helping hand? The Lord will reward you for sure for your kindness."

The truck moved again along the highway raddling its way through the open land. Clouds of smoke trailing behind it then dissipating into the sky above.

"Reverend what are you doing out here? Enoch asked.

"Well my brother, I am a man who is trying to spread the word to a dying planet."

"What's the word? Robert asked.

"What's the word? My brother it's time for everyone to get ready for the end of time."

"End of time? Enoch stated.

"Yes sir, He's going to come down from Heaven and gather us all up and takes us to the Kingdom in the sky. Well maybe not everyone, but I'm sure ready to go. Say you got any water to drink?

Caleb laughed as he listens to the Reverend and then handed him one of the bottles of water. The Reverend was a short but stocky man. Balding with thick dark hair around his head. His black suit was about a size to small and his belly stuck out from under his shirt. His eyes were jet black and his collar was not attached and hung loose. He had no socks only black shoes which had worn soles.

"I don't know about you preacher man. There's something funny about you. I don't think you're telling us everything." Enoch stated.

"Why brother, why would you say such a thing? You can see that I'm certainly a man of the cloth."

"Are you okay back there? Andy shouted to those in the back. "If we pick up any more people, we're going to need a bigger truck."

They traveled on for the biggest part of the day without seeing anyone else along the way. The open terrain was desolate and dry. The sky grew darker and the smell in the air drew their attention the weather.

"I think it's going to get wet soon. We may need to park

and find us a place for the rest of the day." Andy shouted out to those in the back.

"I know a place. When you get to the next intersection that has a stack of rocks turn to the right and follow the road. I'll tell when to stop." Enoch shouted out.

"Where you taking us? Caleb asked.

"I once worked at a place for several days before they sealed it up. It was owned by the military. It was like a warehouse of all kinds of military stuff." Enoch explained. "Here, turn here."

Andy turned at the intersection. A large pile of boulders stood at the intersection. Once the background of a large sign. Andy followed the paved road until the road ended. "Okay, we just ran out of road. All I see are these rolling hills. What now? He asked.

Enoch jumped down from the truck and walked to the front of the truck and viewed the surrounding landscaping. The rolling hills were as dry and barren as the valleys they traveled through.

"What are you looking for? Caleb asked.

"Well, I'll know it when I see it." Enoch replied as he continued viewing the terrain. He started to walk to the other side of the truck then stopped.

"There, over there." He shouted.

Everyone looked in that direction and was silent for several seconds."

"What are we looking at? Caleb asked.

"There, over there." Enoch repeated and began to hurry to the base of the hillside. "Over here, help me move these rocks."

"Move all these rocks? Robert asked.

"Come on, help me." He repeated. "You too preacher."

They began lifting and rolling the mound of rocks that were stacked against the side of the small mountain. After twenty minutes the pile was removed and there before them was what appeared to be a metal door embedded into the mountain. It was a wide door. Rusted and dented, but appeared to be secure.

"We need something to pry it open with. Do you have any tools of some kind that we can wedge open the door? He asked.

"I got a crow bar." Andy stated as he went back to the truck and reached under the seat and removed the crow bar.

He handed the crow bar to Enoch as he tried to pry open the door. They took turns pushing and prying until finally the rusted door made a cracking sound and became loose. They each grabbed a piece of the door and pulled it open enough to squeeze through. The air was dusty and ash floated in the air.

"What is this place? Robert asked.

"If I remember right, and I was only here for a couple of days helping them move items around before they closed it up, it was some kind of a storage area. But I remember seeing all kinds of stuff."

It was dark with no light. The air was stale and musty smelling and the odor of metal was strong. There used to be a light switch somewhere, but I bet the batteries are dead by now. They moved through the darkness very cautiously until it was so dark they could not see in front of them. Suddenly a dim light lit up the opening. They turned around to see that Andy had pulled the truck up to the front and turned on the truck lights. It was enough to see.

There before them were stacks and stacks of crates, barrels, and items covered with canvas tarps.

"What is this place? Robert stated as he walked over to a barrel along the wall and tried to unscrew the cap. Enoch took the crow bar and placed it just right and loosened the cap enough to remove it.

"Gasoline, this barrel has gasoline in it." Robert shouted out.

"Good," Andy shouted out. "That was going to be our next big problem."

"Let see what else there is here. Everyone take a crate and let's see what we can use." Caleb stated.

Everyone got involved opening crates and lifting the tarps off until they reached the back. Mary had found several lanterns still filled with fluid which allow Andy to turn off the trucks lights. The light from the lanterns provided enough light for everyone to see what was stored.

"What do we have that we can use? Caleb asked.

"Over here are some food rations. Military rations, enough to last us several months." Enoch shouted out. "There are two motorcycles in the back, but I'm afraid they are all rusted. I was hoping they were still good. We could have used them.

"Can you fix them at all? Caleb asked.

"No, everything is seized up tight."

"These crates have clothes. Military clothes, pant, shirts, even socks Reverend." Andy shouted out.

As the day continued they sat in a circle enjoying the days find. They filled themselves with the food rations they found and each found some clothing that fit.

"You know the problem we will have is wearing these

41

clothes. Everyone who sees us will think we are the military and we could be shot at. Not everyone is happy to see the military around." Enoch stated.

"We'll have to deal with that when the time comes." Caleb stated as he gathered up some items. "We can stay here tonight and load up the truck with what we need and reseal the door. We still need some water?

"Reverend, didn't you find anything that fits? Andy asked.

"No, I'm okay the way I am." He replied. "I did get me some socks. I got several pair to take with me"

Caleb walked over to Mary and her son Simon. "Did you find enough items for yourselves and your son? He asked.

"Yes we have enough for us. Food was the most important, we haven't eaten in several days and now we have more than enough." She replied with a smile.

"There are shoes over there in that crate, see if any of them will fit you." Caleb stated.

Robert walked over with a stack of blankets and handed each person several.

"Where did you find these at? Enoch asked.

"The last crate in the back had blankets. They're kind of stinky from sitting so long but there going to keep us warm for the night." Robert stated.

Caleb gathered up some of the wood from the crates and stacked it by the fire. The fire brought warmth inside as a small mist began to fall outside. The odor of the damp dirt and ash drifted through the air. Along the side of the fire the good Reverend was already fast asleep. His snoring was loud and crackly and reminded Caleb of the underground shelter he lived in for so long. The crowded quarters provide a several sounds and sights. The snoring, laughter, and crying are moments in his life he will never forget.

"There are some moments in life that one just can't forget." Caleb stated as the Reverend continued snoring.

CHAPTER 7

As morning drew near, Andy stood by the opening peering out over the desolate land. The mist had stopped and the ground had absorbed with wetness. As the sun tried to break through the cracks of gray clouds, small streaks of sun rays touched the ground. "What the sun touches new life will develop some day." Andy stated as Enoch arrived and stood by his side.

"The old world is gone now," Enoch stated. "A new world is about to begin. Everything has to start over."

"I wonder, did those who started this get what they wanted?

"What do you mean? Enoch asked.

"Well, you blow the world apart, nothing is left. What's the gain in all that? Those that survived, you got to feed and care for them. Cities' are destroyed, you got to rebuild them. Nothing is useful, the land, no water, sickness, death. What's the gain in all that?

"I don't know. Maybe it's just having the power to be able to do it." Enoch replied. "We're having to live in two worlds. What used to be and what going to be."

"Every minute of every day is a struggle to survive. Mary

and her son would have died of hunger or sickness, if we hadn't come along when we did." Andy stated.

"Someday someone needs to explain all of this to me." Andy remarked.

"What do you want to know my good man? The Reverend asked as he came up from behind them. He moved to the opening and looked out into the open land.

"What purpose all this has? Andy repeated.

"History is full of moments like this, maybe not to this magnitude, but with the same ideals." The Reverend replied. "The World has been at war most of its existence. The need for power, wealth, and greed. These things have been around for ages."

"Let's gather what we need so we can go." Caleb shouted out.

Everyone gathered the goods they needed and placed them in the back of the truck. The truck was filled with fuel and two barrel was placed in the back. A tarp was placed over the stored items and tied down to secure them. Before leaving they sealed the door shut and restacked the rocks covering the entrance.

"There, that should do it." Caleb stated.

They moved along the main road passing by abandon vehicles. Some slept in the back as hours passed by. They stopped several times to allow the trucks engine to cool down and to stretch their legs.

"I could sure use a smoke." Andy stated.

"A smoke, you mean a cigarette or a good cigar? Enoch replied.

"Right now, either one would do. I haven't had a good smoke for so long, I can't remember when the last time was."

"Smoking is not good for you." Robert stated.

"No good for you maybe, but for me."

Enoch stepped forward and looked out into the distance. "Is that a dust storm coming this way?

Everyone stopped what they were doing and hurried over to see. A large gray cloud had formed in the distance.

"We need to find shelter now." Caleb shouted.

They quickly hurried to the truck and climbed into the back. Mary and the boy sat with Andy in the front as the truck sped off.

"We need to find the first shelter we can find before the dust storm over takes us." He stated as he stood up in the back and looked over the land as they sped along the highway. Caleb continued to look trying to calculate how close the dust storm was.

"There, over there." Enoch shouted.

Two large construction concrete pipes laid on the ground. Andy swung the truck around and drove to where the pipes were laying. He pointed the truck with the back facing the storm. They all jumped out of the truck and hurried over to the round large concrete construction pipes and hurried inside. Both were laying end to end, 6 feet in diameter and were long enough to hold everyone

"We got here just in time." Caleb stated as the wind picked up and the first of the dust started stirring in the air. The wind howled with a roar around the pipe and the dust and ash thickened like a fog. Darkness filled the sky as the heart of the storm had finally reached their location. They could hear small pieces of rock hitting the outer concrete wall. They covered their faces from the clouds of dust that made its way into the open end of the pipe.

Suddenly there was a dark object that through itself into the pipe. It was difficult to see just what had invaded their space. It laid huddled in one mass and then moved against the curved wall.

"What is that? The Reverend shouted.

"It's not what it is, but who is it." Enoch shouted back.

Everyone remained still. Their faces remained covered, fighting off the dust that thickened in the air as the massive dust and ash storm pounded away at the concrete barrier.

"I think it's starting to let up." Caleb stated.

You could still hear objects hitting the outer walls as the wind continued then became less and then down to a small breeze. The air was still thick and choking as everyone continued to keep their faces covered.

Caleb stood up and walked over to what had entered. He stared down at what appeared to be person. He was covered with a large black coat that had a hood attached that draped over his head. His shoes where wrapped with rages and tied with twine and his pants where torn and ragged.

"You, let me see who you are." Caleb stated as he remained standing in front of him.

At first nothing happened. Then suddenly he began to move. He stood upright, his face remained covered. He was much shorter than Caleb and his size was difficult to tell with the large coat that he wore. Suddenly he swung his arm at Caleb. Caleb moved quickly to avoid being hit. He swung again as Caleb again moved out of the way. Before he could swing again he was grabbed from behind by Enoch. Caleb reached over and pulled away the hood. There, standing in front of him was a woman.

"Say, you're a woman." Enoch shouted out.

"Yeah, so what. Let me go you big goon." She shouted back as she twisted and turned trying to get away.

"Why don't you settle down and we'll let you go? Caleb replied as she continued her efforts to get loose.

"Lady if you don't stop I'm going to put you to sleep," Enoch stated as he wrapped his arm under her chin and pulled tight. She started gasping for air and swinging her arms.

"Stop acting crazy and we'll stop." Caleb stated.

"Okay, Okay," she said in a choking voice as her struggling stopped.

Enoch release his arm around her neck and back away. She slowly turned and faced Enoch, then with one quick kick she placed her foot in a sensitive place. Enoch curled over in pain and backed away and went down.

"Try to choke me will you," She stated as she started to approach Enoch again when something hit her from behind. She fell to the ground and was motionless.

"Lord, I hate the scorn of an angry women, and she is really a scorned woman." The Reverend stated as he walked back to where he was sitting. "Making all that noise and fuss."

"Why preacher, that was really something to see." Andy stated as he laughed.

"Yeah, well, these are hard times and it takes some hard actions. Besides I know who she is and she's been kicking her way across the land."

"Who is she? Mary asked as she went over to her to help her. She pulled away the hood and examined her.

"They call her Crazy Mo. She not all there. At least that how she acts. She has this habit of using her foot rather than her brains. So, she gets herself in a lot of trouble." The Reverend explained. "They probably drove her out her and dumped her off."

"She can't be no more than eighteen or nineteen years old," Mary stated as she continued to help her.

Suddenly she started to move and she opened her eyes and grabbed Mary's arm and pulled it away.

"Don't touch me." She shouted out as she tried to sit up, holding her head with the other hand. "Who hit me? She asked.

"I hit you and if you act crazy again I'll do it again." The Reverend remarked as he shook his finger at her.

"Why it's the good Reverend." She shouted out. "They booted you out as well didn't they?

"Yeah, if you hadn't started acting stupid I might still be there. That's what I get for trying to help you." The Reverend stated.

"Look lady, I don't know what's up with you, but you can either act right, and stay with us or you notice there is no door. You can go." Caleb stated. "Make up your mine."

"You got any water? She asked.

"Give her some water." Caleb replied as Mary handed her a bottle from her coat.

"Where you headed? She asked.

"We're going to the West Coast, California." Mary replied.

"West Coast, that's where I was going." She replied.

"Another one going west." Andy stated as he threw up his hands.

"We can't leave people stranded." Mary stated. "This is my son Simon. What's your name?

"They call me Mo." She replied, as she stood up.

"That's not what they call you. It's crazy Mo." The Reverend remarked back as he moved toward the opening.

The wind had almost come to a stop. The dust and dirt was starting to settle to the ground as the air was beginning to clear. Caleb walked over to the truck. It was covered with dust and dirt and the canvas that covered all the stored items was gone. Blown away by the winds.

"At least everything is still here. Let's clean things up and get out of here. There is another canvas somewhere in here." Caleb stated as everyone came out of the concrete pipe and began cleaning the truck.

Andy got into the truck to make sure that it would start. He turned the ignition and the truck growled and sputtered and then started. Black smoke bellowed out the back as a big cloud.

Everyone loaded into the back with Mary and her son sitting in the front with Andy. Crazy Mo remained standing at the back.

"Well, are you coming with us? Robert asked.

Mo said nothing and just stared at the group. She stepped aside as the truck backed up toward the roadway and then started to pull away. She watched as it started to leave and then decided differently. The group watched as she tried to catch up to the truck as it pulled away. Caleb and Robert reached down and grabbed her arm and pulled her into the back of the truck.

CHAPTER 8

They drove for hours stopping several times to fill the gas tank and let the engine cool down. The roads were somewhat clear of wreckage but some areas were thick with dirt. Off in the distance the rolling hills remained naked of growth but in the higher area small patches of green could be seen.

"I wonder where we are. Mary asked.

"Andy shook his head. "Not sure. We haven't come across anything. Like an old sign or something. We haven't seen another person for some time."

They travel for several more hours until the skies became darker. The day was turning to night and the temperature was starting to change. Not that we need more."

"We need to find a place for the night." Caleb shouted out from the back of the truck.

They traveled around the rolling mountains and saw the remains of a small building. Andy pulled off the road and drove to the front. Everyone watched as Enoch jumped down with his rifle and slowly moved around checking to see if there was anyone around. He returned and tossed the rifle to Robert.

"It's clear." He shouted.

"This place was built with left over wood from

somewhere. Look how it was put together." Enoch stated as he walked around the interior. "It's not that old."

They settled down for the night. The building was just a shell. The floor was dirt and there was no glass in the window opening. The Reverend and Robert went about gathering some wood and found enough to start a fire for warmth. They used several of the crates as seats and opened the crate that contained rations. Each received a ration package.

"I know you guys aren't the military." Mo stated. "This guy is too old to be in the military." As she pointed to Andy.

Everyone started laughing as Andy gave Mo a scouring look." You like riding in my truck? He asked as everyone laughed at the sight of Andy's face.

"What are you doing wondering around? Mary asked. "You got any family anywhere?

"Nope. Lost everyone." She replied. "I've been wondering around for some time now.

"Did we bring those crates of shoe and clothes? Caleb asked.

"It's in the back of the truck." Robert replied.

"Take Mo and see if there's anything there that will fit her."

Robert jumped up and waved to Mo to follow him out to the truck. Mo climbed up and helped Robert move the crates until he found the crate that was marked. Mo went through the clothes picking out what she needed.

"You need to leave." Mo stated.

"What for? Robert replied.

"So I can change." She stated...

"Oh, Okay," as he jumped down from the truck and stood by the building waiting for Mo.

Within a few minutes she jumped down and walked toward Robert. He stared at her as her appearance had changed.

"Boy, do you look different." Robert stated.

"Yeah, I'm glad to have some shoes, even if they are these boots." Mo stated as she pointed down to the boots.

"Did you get some of those socks? He asked.

"First thing I put on."

"The first thing? Robert stated.

Once again the good Reverend was already sleeping. His snoring was loud and deep and at times he choked and he rolled over on his side.

"Keep him like that will you." Andy stated.

"Where did you find the Reverend? Mo asked.

"On the road. He waved us down. You know him? Enoch asked.

"Yeah, I know of him. He was with a group of people I was with. I don't know where he came from. He was there when I got there. He was always preaching something and being converted was not what that group was about. They got tired of him fast and he was quickly run out of the group. I guess they took him and dumped him just like they dumped me."

"So why did they dump you? Robert asked.

"I was hungry, all I wanted was a little food. So, one night when they were sleeping I took some. I got caught. They slapped me around. And I guess I used my foot to many times, so they tied me up and dumped me out in the open. I guess dumping me was better than what some of the others got."

"Did they have any weapons or vehicles? Caleb asked.

"Yeah, they had guns, several old jeeps, and a couple of beat up motorcycles. Mo explained.

"Don't count the good Reverend out. He wasn't afraid. He battled them as well. They tried to search him. He wasn't too happy about that and he did some damage to them. He had a book with a hard cover on it, I think it was a big bible and he used it like a club. He hit one man so hard it broke his nose. He didn't stop until they finally corralled him and then they beat him. I thought they were going to kill him until one of the men stopped them. I think he was the leader of the group."

"Do we have any idea where we are? Mary asked.

"I think we've gone through several states I just don't know which ones. I haven't seen any markers, old signs, anything." Andy stated.

"We need to stay on the main road. We know that it goes from coast to coast." Enoch stated.

"How come we don't see any craters in the ground? Robert asked. "If they dropped bombs there should be some big holes in the ground."

"What they sent over here didn't explode on the ground. It exploded above the ground. Probably several miles above the ground." Caleb stated.

"I don't want to hear about that," Mary stated. "We've had enough talk about what happened. Talk about something else."

"Okay, did you know I once milked cows? Enoch stated. "I had the strongest hands. I was really young. I was wondering around looking for work. It was a small farm and he had fifty to sixty milk cows. His milking machine had broken down. I came along at just the right time. Had to milk by hand until he got it fixed. He didn't need me after that." Enoch stated.

"What about you Andy? Robert asked. "What did you do?

"Let's see. I've done so many different things. I worked in a circus once." Andy stated.

"The circus, I bet that was fun." Little Simon spoke for the first time.

"I took care of the elephants. I fed them, watered them, and the worst part was I had to clean up after them. And let me tell you the last part was the hardest. You know how much them animals can eat."

Everyone listened and then laughed as Andy continued to describe the work he did with the elephants. Caleb looked around and saw the faces of everyone who was listening. At that moment, everyone had forgotten where they were and the smiles on their faces as they laughed at what he was describing provided some peace and brought some unity to the group.

"What about you Caleb? Enoch asked.

"When I was about twelve and delivered these papers to the homes. I had an old bicycle my father had given me. It was a terrible bicycle. It used to get teased all the time."

"What was the matter with it? Robert asked.

"It was a girl's bike." Caleb replied.

"A girl's bike, what were you doing with a girl's bike? Simon asked.

"That's all my dad could get at the time. Anyway. I had

this route I followed each day and I delivered a paper to everyone's house along this route. The problem was when I threw the paper it didn't always land where it was supposed to. There were so many complaints that they took the route away from me."

"But why, what did you do? Little Simon asked.

"I threw a paper through a window once. Some landed on the roof of the house. But the biggest one was when I tossed one and hit the old man sitting in his chair on the porch. It went through whatever he was reading and I think I knocked off his glasses. I didn't last very long." Caleb stated as the group began laughing.

"Don't give Caleb anything to throw, we could get hurt." Andy shouted out.

As the night moved along, each took a turn. Even the two boys got involved and told some story. It was a fun moment in time. And for that short moment they forgot there struggles, hardship and the horror of what had happened.

Everyone except Enoch had dozed off and was sleeping. The fire provided some warmth from the cool night air and the structure of the building was sufficient to keep them safe from unwanted critters. Enoch took the first watch and would be relieved by another until morning arrived.

CHAPTER 9

Robert was the first to open his eyes. When he took a deep breath, it came out as a fog. The morning was colder than usual. He pulled his blankets further up over his head.

"Okay, all you sleeping beauties, it's time to rise," a voice stated as the blankets were jerked off Robert.

"Hey, what's the big idea," Robert shouted as he raises up.

"Let's go, everyone get up," The man shouted.

He was a big man wearing a long furry coat with a hood that covered his head. It was faded and worn and tied in the middle. His face was hidden by some type of pull over cloth that was tied in the back. Only his eyes could be seen. A pair of riding goggles daggled below his chin.

"Caleb jumped up. "Who are you?

"None of your business. You are the first people I've seen for some time. What are you doing in my building? The man stated as he pointed the rifle at the group.

"All of you, against that wall. Let's go, I need to keep all of you in my sights." He shouted out as the group all moved against the wall.

"Where's the Preacher? Andy asked.

"He's here, don't worry. He's just outside resting a little. He had a hard night. So, what's your story? He again asked.

"We needed a place for the night, and we saw this place. We thought it was abandon. We didn't know it belong to anyone." Enoch stated.

"This place belongs to me and you're trespassing. I built this place out the junk I found and I don't rent out any rooms."

Andy leaned over to Caleb and quietly whispered. "Where's Crazy Mo, she's not here."

"I don't know," Caleb replied in a whisper.

"The next thing is what to do with all of you. I could just take you out and shoot you one at a time."

"I know mister," a voice came from behind.

He turned around and suddenly felt a foot that dropped him to his knees. Quickly Enoch grabbed the man's rifle that was dropped.

"You're not going to do anything," Enoch shouted back as he pointed the rifle at the man.

There, standing at the entry was Crazy Mo. She looked at everyone and gave a big smile and then shook her head.

"I go out for just a minute to use the bathroom and you guys get yourself in all kinds of trouble. Who is this guy? She stated.

Robert and Simon ran over to Mo. "Are we glad to see you?" They stated.

"Boy, did you lay this guy out." Robert stated as he watched the man make all kinds of groaning sounds as he laid on the ground.

"We need to find the preacher. He had the last watch last night." Andy stated.

"He's alright. He was tied up outside. I think this guy

caught the good preacher by surprise early this morning." Mo stated.

Andy hurried outside and brought the Preacher in. He walked over to the man lying on the ground. He looked down at him." Hurts doesn't it. Well, here's one from me for jumping me when I wasn't looking." The Reverend stated as he started to give him a kick.

"Hold on Preacher, he's already down," Andy replied as he grabbed the Preachers arm and pulled him back.

"Now, the question is what are we going to do with you? Enoch stated as he watched the man try to get up from the ground. Dirt covered his clothes as he was still in pain.

"We'll be leaving soon and you can have this place back. So, I suggest that you just relax and let us get prepared to leave." Caleb stated.

"A man has to protect what belongs to him." The man stated as he backed off and found a place to sit. "I wasn't going to shoot you or anything like that."

"How are we supposed to know that? Enoch replied back as he kept the rifle on him.

"Besides the rifle hasn't any bullets in it." The man stated.

Enoch checked the rifle and found no bullets in its chamber. He tossed the rifle to the man. He took the rifle and laid it down next to him.

"So, where are you going? The man asked.

"Don't tell him." Andy replied to Caleb. "We'll end up with another passenger."

"Don't worry, I'm not going anywhere. I built this place and here is where I want to stay. Got everything I need." He stated.

"This place is nowhere." Enoch stated.

"What do you mean nowhere? He replied. "There's game and plenty of water."

"What do you mean plenty of water? Caleb asked as they all turned around when they heard the word water.

"There's a small lake about a quarter of a mile away. Just around those small hills."

"Water, we need water. Can you take us there? Caleb asked.

"If you keep that girl away from me while you're here I can. And I mean far away." He stated.

"Mo, leave this guy alone will you? Andy shouted out to Mo.

"Tell him to be good and I'll stay far away from him." She replied.

"You know, this will be a good time for someone to take a bath."

"Who needs a bath? Andy replied.

"Probably everyone. When was the last time anyone of you had the opportunity to bathe? Caleb asked.

"I don't know what he's talking about." Andy replied as he walked outside.

They gathered their items and loaded the truck and followed the man's directions. The truck moved along the dirt road and then rounded the small hills to the right. There along the side of the hill was a sight they hadn't seen in a long time. Andy pulled the truck to the edge and parked it. Everyone jumped down and hurried to the lakes edge. It was a sight they had not seen since before the big event took place. The water was a light blue and around its edges were small green scrubs. Spotted in some areas were the beginnings of new growth as trees that were totally barren at one time had signs of green leaves dotted on their branches.

"Look at this," Robert shouted as he pointed to the few new creatures that moved about. "Look over there." He pointed as two small cranes rose up from the water's edge and spread their wings, then flew to a new spot along the waters shallows.

"How long has this been here? Caleb asked.

"It's been here for a while. It used to be much larger than this. Probably three time the size. But this is what's left. And the water has cleaned itself. I don't think the fish are big enough right now to even bother with. But some day they will be back to the size." The man stated.

"Let's stay here for a while? Robert asked.

"Yeah, we need to get some things done." Enoch stated as he looked at Andy.

CHAPTER 10

They spent the day at the lake. Enoch had convinced Andy that this would be a good time for a dip in the water. They had no soap but water would at least help the situation. Robert and Simon played around in the water's shallows, pushing one another and enjoying the freshness of the water. Even the preached enjoyed the water and found the time to wash his clothes. Robert and Simon laughed when they saw the preacher remove his shirt and begin to wash it. His big belly fell out over his pants.

'What are you two laughing at? He asked.

"Nothing," Robert shouted back as the boys snickered at the sight of the preacher.

Each person took some time out to make themselves presentable. The water was not cold but had a warmth to it.

"What makes this water feel warm? Caleb asked.

"I think there must be some underwater thermal something going on. As barren as the land is you would think that the land would suck this water up. But it continues to remain this size and temperature. In fact, I think it's getting larger." The man stated as he put his hand into the water.

After several hours, they prepared to camp alongside the water's edge. A small fire provided heat to dry their clothes.

Some sat around the edge of the fire while others took the time to catch up on some needed sleep.

"We never got your name? Enoch asked.

"My name is Abram." He replied.

"What are you doing out here?

"I've been out here for some time. I ran across this place and just decided this was as good as any. I started collecting materials and began building the framework of that shack you spent the night in." Abram stated. "Where are you headed for?

"I think we all started out going in different directions until we ran across one another, now we're headed for the west coast. Caleb is trying to find his father there, and the rest of us are tagging along." Enoch stated. "Are there any others that come here?

"No one has been here other than all of you. Most of the animals come here to drink throughout the day. Other than that, no one. Where did you get those military clothes?

"We found them some time ago. Do you need some clothes?

"I could sure use a change." He remarked.

"I'll get you some." Enoch replied.

The day was fading away as the night slowly filtered its way in. In the morning, they made their way back to the shack. The truck bounced around as it moved along the dirt path as they followed their tire tracks when suddenly the truck stopped.

"What's the matter? Caleb said from the back of the truck.

"There, look there." Andy stated.

Everyone stood up from the back of the truck to see.

There at the shack was a jeep. Two men were walking around the building. Each had a weapon in their hands. Their heads were covered with a cloth hood and they both wore some type of black leather looking coat. They moved very slowly being careful. They both stopped and examined the ground looking at the prints in the dirt.

"What are they doing? Robert asked.

"I think they found our tracks." Caleb remarked.

Suddenly Abram jumped down from the back.

He began to walk to the front of the truck.

"Where are you going? Andy asked.

"I'll take care of this," he stated. "All of you stay here and no matter what you see, stay here. Do you understand?

Everyone nodded as they watched him walk toward the visitors. At first they didn't see him, then they quickly saw him approaching. They began yelling and shouting at him as Abram raised his arms over his head. Their weapons were drawn as they moved toward him.

"Here over here, keep your hands where I can see them." The smaller one shouted. The other man moved behind Abram and began pushing him forward. When he reached their jeep, the bigger man pushed him to the ground. Abram fell hard landing face down.

"This your place? He asked.

Abram raise up, "Yeah this is my place."

"Anyone else here?

"No, just me." He replied as he tried to raise up from the ground.

"You building this place? The short one asked.

"Yeah, I'm building this place."

"If you're going to live here you're going to have to pay some rent. Got any money? He asked.

"No, got no money." He replied.

"Got anything to trade?

"No."

"Well, I guess were just going to have to shoot you." The small one stated as he pointed his weapon at Abram.

The other laughed as he lowered his weapon and walked up to Abram and raised him to his feet. With one quick move, he used the butt of the weapon to hit Abram in his mid- section. Abram curled over and dropped to his knees. He grabbed Abram and raised him to his feet again and this time through a punch to the side of Abram face. He fell backwards to the ground again. Blood began dripping from his nose and the side of his face began to swell. The other man laughed as he leaned on the jeep watching the beating take place.

"Nothing free." The man said as he hit Abram again. And again, he fell to the ground. "I think it's your turn. The one man said to the other. He laughed and placed his weapon on the hood of the jeep and walked over to Abram and grabbed him.

'Now this is what we're going to do. We don't want to be unreasonable about things, so I think we'll just burn your place down.". He stated as he hit Abram in the mid-section, then watched him fall against the outer wall of the shack.

"You know what, we don't have time for this. Get out of the way let me shoot this guy so we can go."

Abram dropped to the ground. The shorter man turned to get his weapon from the hood of the jeep and stopped.

"Where's my ....Suddenly one shot rang out hitting

the man and lifting him off the ground and tossing him against the building. The other man turned quickly and began to fire wildly into the distance. Another shot was fired hitting the other man as he dropped to the ground.

"Abram laid still on the ground. He had taken what they gave him and said nothing of the others. He pulled himself up and leaned against the building outer wall. Quickly as it happened Enoch arrived and help Abram.

"Someone is a good shot? Abram stated as he wiped his face.

"Andy is a cracker jack at long range. Two shots, two down." Enoch stated as he helped Abram inside and sat him down. The rest of the group hurried over as they could hear the truck coming from where it was parked.

"How is he? Caleb asked.

"He'll be alright." Enoch replied.

"You know they would have shot me and then burn this place down? Abram stated.

"I know it. If they would have found us, we would have been in the same place I'm afraid." Caleb stated. "We need to take care of things before it gets any darker. "Come on preacher, I need your help. We need to dispose of these guys."

"You can say a few words over them."

"I don't think I want to say anything over these two knowing where there going." The Reverend stated as he helped Caleb.

CHAPTER 11

They removed the bodies of the two men and found a place to bury them. They stay busy throughout the day and decided to stay another night. As the night closed in and the darkness filled the space the group remained inside the shack. A small fire was burning in the middle providing some light and warmth.

"We need to leave in the morning. Are you going to be alright? Caleb asked.

"Yeah, I'll be okay. I'm going to take down this place and move it to the other side of the hills closer to the water"

"Listen, we'll help you in the morning. We can load this on the truck and move it for you. It shouldn't be that hard to take down and move." Caleb stated. "If we all help it shouldn't take no more than a couple of hours."

"Why did you build it here instead of by the water? Enoch asked.

"Most of the wood was here and I didn't find the lake till after I had most of it built. But now I need to get it closer to the water." Abram explained.

The morning was cool as always. The sun tried its best to break through the cloud cover but only slivers of sun light could touch the ground. Slowly each person began to awake and move around until the entire group was now moving about and preparing their items for another day on the road.

They placed their items outside the shack and began the task of removing the wood sidings and placing them on the truck. The wall came down quickly until the entire shack was now loaded into the truck. Andy drove the truck while the others walked. Mo and Mary rode inside with Andy.

It didn't take long before they reached the spot where Abram wanted to rebuild his shack. The others finally reached the spot and they all began the task of unloading the materials. They laid each wall exactly where Abram wanted to reassembly the shack.

"That's good," Abram stated as he overlooked the layout of materials. "I can take it from here. I need to make it a little more solid than before."

"We need to get going," Caleb stated as they all said their goodbyes. "If we ever come by this way again we'll be sure to stop by. We'll leave you the jeep. Be careful with it and keep it out of site. You never know, they might be looking for it."

They loaded onto the truck and made their way back picking up their items. The ride back to the main road took only a few minutes as the truck once again clanked and sputtered its way along. Smoke barreling out the back.

"With all the smoke bellowing out the back, does this thing ever run out of oil? Enoch asked.

"Andy seems to have it in control. I see him tinkering with it each day we've stopped. Guess he's taking care of things." Caleb remarked back.

Several hours had passed as their journey continued. Mo and Mary kept Andy entertained inside the cab while the others talked and took naps in the back. The landscaped began to change. More and more objects appeared alongside the road and from a distance ruins of buildings could be seen.

"We must be getting closer to a city. There is more junk laying around. Enoch stated as he stood up hanging on the wooded rails of the truck.

"Did you notice the further we go west the warmer it gets? Caleb stated. "The sun is breaking through the clouds."

Suddenly the truck began to slow down as its brakes squealed until it came to a stop. Caleb stood up and looked over the railing.

"Why are we stopping? He asked

"Up ahead," Enoch replied. "We've run out of road."

"How can we run out of road? The Reverend stated as he too stood up and looked over the railing.

Andy climbed out of the truck's cab and stood looking. There before them was a crater. The pavement was gone and deep crater appeared. At the bottom of the crater water had formed from an underground stream.

"Look at that," Robert stated as everyone stood gazing into the opening.

"That, my friend will be a lake soon." Caleb stated as they all stood at the edge of the crater. "The only way we can keep moving is to go around this."

"There was a dirt road a mile or two back." Andy stated. "Let's go."

"Why don't we just follow the edge of the lake till we get around it? The Reverend ask.

"We don't know what kind of soil is out there. We

could get stuck and we can't afford that." Andy stated as he climbed back inside the cab. "Let's get going." He shouted.

The truck turned around and followed the road back until a dirt road was visible. The truck kicked up more dust and dirt as the soil was loose but was solid enough to travel on. Other tracks appeared in the dirt and soon the outline of other vehicles appeared. Some stripped and others appeared operational. Andy slowed the truck down then stopped. He shouted to those in the back.

"You might want to have your rifles ready. Don't know what's up ahead." He shouted.

Caleb and Enoch lifted the canvas that covered their supplies and each took a weapon. As the truck got closer they could see movement ahead.

"Everyone stay down. We don't know what's ahead of us. If we start shooting be sure to stay down." Caleb ordered. "Here Reverend take this," as Caleb handed him a rifle.

"Look up ahead." Andy shouted as the truck began to slow down.

"It looks like a check point of some kind. These guys are wearing uniforms." Enoch stated.

The truck slowed down even more and then stopped. Four men in uniforms surrounded the truck.

"Who are you and where are you going? The one solder asked as the others walked around inspecting the truck.

"We're traveling west. We had to come this way because of the giant hole in the ground." Andy stated.

"What are you carrying? He asked again as the others examined the truck and those in the back.

"Just some travelers heading in the same direction." He replied.

"What's under the canvas?

"Why do you need to know? The Reverend shouted out from the back.

"This is a secure town. We need to know who's wanting in."

"These are out supplies." Caleb stated.

"Why are you wearing those uniforms? Where did you get them? He asked.

"We found them and we needed some clothes. Let's skip the questions. Where are we? Caleb demanded.

"This is station 5, check point Outer Limits." The one soldier stated.

"Outer Limits of what? Enoch asked.

"Outer Limits of New Haven." He replied.

"What's New Haven? The Reverend asked.

"A newly formed city which is located about a mile up the dirt road. Now let us check your vehicle." He remarked as the other soldiers climbed into the back and examined the contents of the truck.

"It's just crates and other stuff." The one soldier stated as they climbed down.

"Where did you get the weapons?

"From a couple of bad guys who decided they wanted what we had." Enoch replied.

"What happened to them?

"Well, let's just say they have a new career now." Enoch stated.

"Okay, here's the rules you need to follow. New Haven is a military city. It is heavily guarded. You're welcome to enter or travel through it, but put the weapons away. Store them. Is that understood?

"Understood." Andy replied.

They lifted the barrier as Andy pulled the truck pass the check point and followed the dirt path. As they moved closer they could see the outline of canvas tents. Some were small while others were large. People were moving about and many stopped when they saw the truck entering. The truck slowly moved closer until it reached another check point. More soldiers surrounded the truck.

"Here we go again." Andy shouted out.

"You need to pull your vehicle over to the south end. There you will be directed where to go. No weapons.

"Which way is South? Andy asked.

The soldier pointed, "That way."

Andy followed the direction and soon they were driving into a large area where many larger vehicles were parked. Another soldier directed them to a specific spot. Andy shut the engine down and climbed out of the cab. Mary and Mo also got out and met with those in the back. Four more soldiers walked up to them, each carrying weapons.

"You need to follow us." The one soldier stated.

"Where we going? Caleb asked.

"You need to be cleared from the medical group before entering the city. Follow us and we can get this done. Don't worry, no one will bother your stuff. There are eyes watching everywhere."

They followed the soldiers into a large canvas tent where several others were waiting as well. Soldiers where directing people to different areas inside the large tent. They were directed to seat down and wait. Two soldiers stayed with them.

"Here put these on," The man stated as he handed each

one a tag on a plastic string. "Write your name on the front and place it around your neck. And write big enough so we can read the name.

Enoch looked over at Andy who was examining what was given to him. "Can you write? He asked.

"Yeah I can write." Andy replied.

Enoch laughed as a woman in a white uniform stopped in front of him and asked his name. "I need you full name," she asked.

"You want my name? Enoch replied.

"No his name." She answered.

"His name is Andy." He replied.

"Look stupid, I've been up for 36 hours, let's get this done now." She stated in a voice that meant business.

Each one in the group was questioned and then each was directed to a specific area where they were medically checked. After several hours, they were released into the city.

"You must at all times wear your name tags. Is that understood? Never remove them." The last soldier instructed them as he directed them to the entrance of the city. "Should you decide to leave you must return to that tent over there for departure instructions, is that clear?

They all agreed to the instruction and peer out into the New Haven City.

CHAPTER 12

As they looked over the sights of the City, they were looking into a New World. People were moving about in large groups stopping at different vendor tents. Children were running through the street laughing and dodging others who were moving about. Soldiers in pairs of two were moving about the crowd insuring the safety of others and watching for intruders who might invade the city.

"Wow, look at this." Robert stated as he and Simon jumped in front of the group. "Look at all the people."

Two soldiers stopped. "You people new here? He asked.

"Yeah, we just got here." Enoch stated.

"You can go where you want, but be sure to keep those name tags on. If you're hungry the food tent is just up ahead. You can help yourself. There is a clothing outlet further up if you need some clothes. Where did you get the military clothes?

"We found them," Caleb stated. "Let's go and eat."

They walked slowly through the crowded lane viewing each of the tents as they passed them. Some had items of clothing and others had small trinkets. There were gathering places where individuals would sit and just talk with others.

They could smell the food in the air as they reached the

food tent. Two soldiers were standing at the entry as they walked up.

"You want to eat? He asked.

"Are you kidding," Enoch replied as he looked over at the table that was covered with different food items.

"Here, you'll need one of these. Each time you come to eat they will punch a hole in the card for that day. Keep these with you," he stated as he handed each person a card that was attached to their I, and placed around their neck.

It was a large tent with several tables in the front with several round table and chairs scattered throughout the space for sitting. They each took a tray and followed the line of people who were there to eat as well. Attendants behind the food tables would service each person. When they reached the end of the line they were directed to a table.

Robert and Simon hurried to the table eating along the way as they all could sit together. Other individuals at different table stopped to see who had just entered near them. Everyone seemed suspicious of new comers. It didn't take long before everyone settled down and resumed eating and their conversations.

"What is this? Reverend asked as he examined his plate.

"Who cares? Andy stated back.

"It's some kind of process meat I think. Here, put some of this on it. It like BBQ sauce I think." Mo stated as she passed the container to the Reverend...

"We can get some new clothes. The clothing tent is just across from us. It would be best if we ditch these military clothes." Caleb stated. "When we finish, let's go over there and see what they got."

"We need to find a place to sleep." Mary stated. I could use a soft bed if they got such a place."

"Me too." Simon replied with a stuffed mouth.

"I wonder where all this comes from," Andy remarked as he looked around the room at all the people eating. Tables were filled with individuals and others appeared to be families.

"These are all survivors who came here just like you folks," a man stated walking up behind them. "I'm Captain C.J Wilson. I am currently the commanding officer of this center. Did you just arrive? He asked as he walked around the table.

"We just arrived several hours ago." Enoch stated as he continued to eat. "We just came from the medical examiners.

"Did you receive your shots? He asked.

"Yes, each of us got our shots and they hurt? Robert stated.

"What's your name? The Captain asked.

"That's the President," Enoch stated.

"The President of what? He asked with some confusion.

"The President." Enoch replied as he leaned back in his chair and wiped his mouth. "He's the last remaining family member of the great George Washington."

"This kid?

"Yep. So, if I was you, and I'm glad I'm not. I'd be very careful what I say to such a distinguished public servant."

"The honor is mine then." The Captain stated as he snapped to attention and saluted Robert.

Robert continued eating not paying much attention to what Enoch as said. He was used to his teasing moments and decided he wasn't worth the battle.

The Captain directed them to the area of housing and instructed them on what was needed. When they finished eating they walked through the crowd and crossed the street to the clothing outlet. Inside, they were greeted by another soldier who directed them to another individual who would assist them in selecting the appropriate clothing. Each received what was needed and was then asked to change and deliver their old clothing to the bins near the back.

"All the old clothing from the old world needs to be destroyed. We try to keep everything clean." The one attendant stated.

"I'm a man of the cloth." The Reverend stated. "I need to keep my attire."

"Sorry padre, the old stuff got to go."

"Preacher you look like you should be selling cars." Enoch stated as everyone laughed when the Reverend came out from the dressing area. His pants were faded and his shirt was a combination of different colors.

They left the clothing outlet and continued walking through the crowded street. It seemed to get thicker as the day went along and it became difficult to move with so many people.

They reached a large tent with a number 24 painted on the outside. That was the location of the sleeping quarters which the soldier had told them about. This tent was like most of the others, all aligned in a row, each with a number on the outside. Inside, row of cots filled the interior. A soldier and several attendants greeted them as they entered. They were directed to a row of cots in the back of the tent. They each found an empty cot as another attendant presented each of them with several blankets and a towel. They were each handed a small box which contained their health items, soap, toothbrush, and other needed items.

The men were directed to stay together and the women were asked to stay in another area not far from the others. Around them other families were housed as children ran through the aisles and babies cried in the distance.

"I sure hope I can sleep with all this noise." Andy stated and he prepared his bed. "For some reason I'm really tired."

"I could sleep in the middle of the road." Enoch replied as he threw himself onto the cot and wrapped the blankets around him. He pulled the hat he was given over his face.

"Aren't you going to take your shoes off? The Preacher asked.

"Nope." He replied, "The shoes stay on my feet."

Within seconds everyone was sleeping even with all the noise that was around them. They remained asleep through the balance of the day and through the night until morning.

By early morning Caleb was stirring. He raised up and then removed the blankets and sat up in the cot. Others were still sleeping and the tent was filled with the sounds of others doing the same. Several soldiers walked around keeping a watchful eye. Caleb watched as they passed by. They were dressed in full battle uniform with side arms and didn't talk to anyone while on their patrol. They were always in pairs, and had ear pieces which allowed them to communicate with someone.

As the morning started to fall into place the others were up and moving about. Mary and Mo had found several others to talk to and Robert and Simon were still sleeping. The Reverend had found several others that needed his uplifting words. Andy seems satisfied with sleeping the day away and Enoch approached Caleb and sat down next to him.

"How long do you want to stay here? He asked.

"I don't know, maybe long enough for us to catch up on things and find out what happening in other places." He replied.

"Everyone seems pretty content right now. The boys have found others to talk to and the ladies are busy with their own group. I guess we should let everyone do their own thing for a while."

"I heard there is a meeting this morning. It's update on what's going on. I think I'll go to it and find out what's happening." Enoch stated.

"We'll both go. Andy will probably want to check on his truck. I don't think he's comfortable leaving it where he parked it. I don't think he trust some of these people." Caleb stated as he stood up and stretched. "Let's gather those that want to go and eat."

They walked through the large tent to the outside street and noticed another eating area close by. The street was busy and people were moving about. By later in the day the street would be filled with people and the day would be totally underway.

The street was not paved but lined with very small gravel bits and were contained by wood edgings. There were men doing many different tasks, some were gathering up loose items on the ground. Others were ensuring the receptacles were emptied. Several men wore an orange jump suit and were making repairs on the tents. The City of New Haven was fully organized into work details and secured by the Countries military.

"Where's Andy? Caleb asked.

"Still sleeping I guess. That's where he was when we left."

CHAPTER 13

They entered the tent and stopped as a man approached them. He was tall, young and very well dressed. His hair was dark, well groomed, and around his neck was an ID card with his picture displayed.

"You here for the meeting? He asked.

"Yeah, this is the place right? Caleb asked as he looked around. The space was already filling with those that wanted to know what was happening with the world they lived in.

"Take a seat, we'll start in just a few minutes." He stated as he greeted others who were arriving. They found seat midway and looked around to see if there was anyone they might know. People from all over migrated to the New Haven when they heard there was a place for survivors. Hundred filtered in from far away as the Government was trying to restart the country.

"Ladies and Gentlemen please welcome Major Henry Cole." The young captain introduced.

"Thank you and welcome. I wanted to personally tell you that across the country cities like this one are forming and citizens of this great nation are coming together. So, you are not alone. As the environment begins to change we will increase our ability to produce what is necessary to sustain us. I also want to tell you that our armed forces are organized and ready to assist in all phases of the rebuilding process and that we have gained control of our national defense system."

The crowd was excited at what was said and began clapping.

"Does this mean we can go back to our homes and began to rebuild our lives? One man from the back shouted out.

"Yes. Our scientific community believes we are no longer in danger of any radiation and to add to the good news, our water is clearing and we hope to see the sun as it was." He stated.

The crowd got excited again, cheered and began clapping again

"What about the groups of outlaws that continue to plaque us, rob us and take what little we have? Another man shouted out.

"As we speak this day, the military at the orders of the President of the United States has directed all of its armed forces to protect it citizens and to round up all of those who are engaged in this kind of action against its citizens. This might take some time but we will ensure you everything is being done to make this happen."

"Looks like we came here at the right time." Enoch stated. Suddenly Robert ran into the tent and whispered something into Caleb ear. Caleb jumped up and hurried out the tent ran to the sleeping area. A crowd had gathered as they watched several Government men moving about inside the tent.

"Sir, you need to stay out here," The soldier stated as he held Caleb back.

"That's my sleeping area and that's my friend." Caleb replied as he pulled the arm away that was holding him and he ran inside. One soldier ran after him until he reached the cots. Caleb stopped short as two medical staff stood up and began to talk.

"This guy is gone," the one stated as he placed his medical tools back into his bag.

"That's my friends there, what's the matter with him? Caleb asked.

"I'm sorry sir, this man has passed away. It appears he's been died for some time. Probably last night. You need to let these men do their job so they can remove him. We're very sorry for you lose. Did he have any relatives or friends anywhere?

"Only us." Caleb stated. "Only us."

Caleb stepped aside to allow the men to remove Andy's body. He was peacefully asleep just as he was last night. Caleb left and hurried back and met the others coming his way. He waved them over to the side of the street.

"What's the matter? Robert says there's something wrong with Andy? Mo stated.

"There is, big time I'm afraid." He replied.

"Well tell what it is." Mary asked.

"Andy passed away in his sleep last night. They just came for him.

"What do you mean," Reverend asked. "He's gone? I can't believe it, he had so much energy."

"Well you can believe it now. He's gone. I got the keys to the truck. Let's go somewhere and talk." Caleb replied.

They followed Caleb to an area that seemed clear from the crowd. "I need to move on. I need to see if my father made it, so I'm going to leave in the morning. If any of you wish to go with me that okay, but if you would rather stay here that's okay as well. At least you'll be cared for while you're here. Think about it overnight and let me know because I'm leaving in the early morning."

The balance of the day seemed to speed along and they all had reached a decision that night. As they met in the dining area to eat it was very quiet. They seemed to be interested in who was going to speak first with their decision.

"I don't want to wait till the morning to tell you, Simons and my decision. I need to think about Simon's life and make that my priority. We will stay here. But I want you to know that you saved our lives. We would have never survived there on our own if it hadn't been for all of you." Mary stated with a sad expression on her face as she looked at each person at the table. "I wish Andy was here. We used to talk in the truck."

"That's probably the right decision." Caleb stated.

"I think I'm going to stay too." The Reverend stated. "There's much I can do here and Andy is in a better place."

"Reverend I thought you were the adventurist type? A good battle or two was right up your alley." Enoch stated.

"No, I've had enough of those battles. It's time to get this World back on track." He replied. "I'll leave the battles to you. But I want to wish you the very best in finding your father."

"That's good. I thought you might want to stay." Caleb remarked. "What about you Mo. What's you plan?

"Me? She asked.

"No, the women sitting behind you, yes you." Enoch stated. "What do you want to do?

"I've thought about it and I think I'll tag along with you. I've always wanted to see the ocean. Is there still an ocean?

"I'm sure there's still an ocean." He replied.

"No one asked me yet so I'm going to tell you. I'm going too. I've made it this far, might as well go the distance." Robert said with a full mouth.

"I wonder, did your decision to go have anything to do with that question they asked you when we got here about going to school? Enoch asked.

"Oh no, not at all." Robert replied, as he stared into his plate.

"What about you Enoch. You haven't said anything yet?

"I took some time to think about it. It was a difficult decision to stay or go." He remarked. "But I think I'll go as well. I'm not that fond of large crowds of people and I'd like to see the ocean as well.

"You took all of a few minutes to make up your mind," the Reverend stated.

"Now there you go Reverend, saying such negative things." Enoch stated as he laughed as did everyone at the table.

"Alright, we be leaving in the early morning." Caleb stated. "We'll say our goodbyes tonight."

It was quiet the rest of the time. Everyone stayed to themselves. They caught up on some sleep while others talked and spoke of Andy.

CHAPTER 14

That night everyone said their goodbyes. They watched in the early morning as the truck sped away through the city and out past the outer limit posts. The truck was again the attention of everyone as it clanked and sputtered in a cloud of black smoke. Caleb drove as Mo sat inside with Robert and Enoch in the back. It seemed a little strange not having the others with them. They had gone through some difficult times together and it just felt a little lonely.

They drove for several hours and had gone through some very rough terrain. They had driven around the crater following other tracks in the dirt. And Caleb was instructed by those in New Haven about the directions he needed to follow and the warnings of being out in the open. He eventually found the paved road again and was back on a smooth surface. As they traveled once again the old-world relics were displayed throughout the landscape. And at times they would have to pull off the road and drive around some rusted wreckage that blocked there way. Hours had passed when the first sight from a distance gave them some hope.

"What is that mountain range there? Mo asked. As she leaned forward to look at what appeared to be a long set of mountains that reached out in both directions.

"I believe those are the Serra Nevada Mountains. Look at the green that is growing at the top." Caleb stated.

"So does that mean we're in Nevada? She asked.

"Well, I'd say we probably have been for some time now," He stated.

"Nevada, it's the State with all the casino's? Mo asked again.

"Yep, I believe that's the State." He replied.

"I wonder if we'll see anything like that. She asked.

"Once we get closer to the border towns we might see something, but don't be discouraged if it's in bad shape like every other place we've come to." Caleb stated.

"Hey Caleb," Enoch shouted from the back. "There's a bunch of vehicles coming from behind us and I think they're in a big hurry."

Caleb slowed down and looked out the back to see what appeared to be a group of vehicles, mostly trucks heading their way. He continued on but at a much slower pace and stayed to the right side to allow them to pass, hoping that passing was on their agenda. As they pulled up behind the truck, through its cloud of black smoke, they honked several times and then sped past, as each truck took its turn passing by. The last vehicle was a jeep which pulled up along-side as Caleb slowed down then stopped. Four soldiers sat inside the jeep, all armed with automatic weapons. The soldier closest to Caleb leaned over and shouted.

"You might want to pull over for the night. There is an armed conflict with some of the criminal element up ahead. We have them cornered but we don't want any civilian casualties. There's a site up head about a mile. A road off to the right. Take it and stay the night. Someone will come by and let you know when it's clear."

Caleb waved and watched as the jeep sped away. Enoch and Robert were standing on the rails watching.

"What's up? Enoch asked.

The military is fighting the bad guys up ahead. They told us to park for the day. There is a place up ahead that we can stay for the night."

Caleb followed the road until he reached the turn off, pulled off and followed it for several miles until he reached an area where others were resting and waiting. Small tents were erected and fires were burning.

"This looks like a good place for the night." Caleb stated as he pulled the truck into the area away from the rest of those parked.

"Why didn't you park the truck over there closer to those people? Robert asked.

"We don't know who's in here. Once we know the place is okay, you can go visiting." Caleb stated. "We can stay in the back of the truck tonight. We can take the tarp and make a cover and we have lots of blankets." Caleb stated.

"What's that smell? Enoch stated.

"I think someone is cooking." Mo stated as she started to walk toward the others.

"She really listens." Caleb stated. "Keep an eye on her while I get Robert to fill the trucks tank with some gas. It will be dark soon.

"Now where you going? Enoch asked as he watched Robert follow Mo.

"With her." He replied. "Can you smell that?

"No one follows directions around here, wait for me? He stated as he hurried and caught up with Robert and Mo.

The group they met was a man and his wife. They had a large pot that was cooking over an open fire.

"Hello there, we can't help but smell what you're cooking from over there." Enoch stated as he pointed to their location.

"Why did you park so far away? She asked.

"We were just being careful." Robert replied. "What is that smell?

"It's a stew that been brewing for most of the day. It's got lots of real vegetables and it even has some meat in it. This is my husband Charlie and I'm his wife Iris."

"My name is Enoch; this is Mo and this guy is the President."

"The President of what? She asked.

"The big guy."

"What big guy." Charlie replied.

"No one knows who the big guy is? He's the last remaining decedent of George Washington." Enoch stated

"You got to be kidding," Charlie remarked. "Really?

"Well that's what he says."

Charlie was an older man in his fifties and his wife Iris matched that age as well. They traveled in an old rusted RV with patches of different color paint applied in different areas.

"How come it has so many colors? Robert asked.

I just couldn't make up my mind. Still can't decide what color I like." Charlie stated. "You guys want to stay and eat with us? We got plenty.

"You bet we do." Robert remarked as he found a place to sit.

"Who are the rest of the people over there? Enoch asked.

"There a Mexican family. Don't speak much English. They like to keep to themselves. I think there a little afraid of other people. They're traveling in the same direction as we are. Into California, when we got stopped by the Military and told we needed to hangout here for a while. So here we are and here we'll stay."

"Well I see that we are all happily enjoying our time." Caleb stated as he joined the group. "I'm Caleb.

The night arrived and in the distance one could see the lights flashing as the battle was taking place. At times, there was a great amount of lights but slowly it disappeared.

"Well, I think that battle is coming to an end. We used to hear the loud sounds of guns but that disappeared as well." Charlie described.

"Is everyone ready to eat? Iris stated as she began dishing out bowls of the stew that had been cooking most of the day.

"So where are you headed if you don't mine me asking? He asked.

"Into California. I'm looking for my father. He lived near San Francisco. I haven't seen him since things started happening."

"He lived underground." Robert stated as he filled his mouth with bits of potatoes.

"We did also for many years. When we found out we could come out, we did just that." He explained. "We found this old RV parked behind a large concrete wall. I guess the wall was thick enough to protect it. I got this old RV to run and here we are. Iris's sister has lived in the bay area all her life. We're hoping she's still there."

"What are you going to do if she not there? Mo asked.

"Well, I think this is the end of the road for us. We'll try to make our home there." Charlie explained. "They say there is a large military presence there. And there might be a lot of work available with the Government restoring the citied.

"Say, isn't this the place where actors come who want to be in politics? Enoch asked. "Wasn't there a couple of them, I can't think who it was. I remember someone talking about it once."

"That was a long time ago." Charlie replied with a smile.

The night moved along with some quiet conversation and but not everyone was listening. Robert who had stuffed himself was now sleeping.

"Does the boy belong to you? Charlie asked.

"No. He lived on the streets when I ran across him. He got me out of the city and through the mountains. He's very street smart." Caleb stated.

"He's not afraid. He'll battle if he needs to." Enoch added. "The one you got to watch out for is this lady next to me."

Mo looked over at Enoch, "Will you be quiet." Mo stated as they all chuckled.

"This is a harsh environment. Everyone needs to be able to take care of themselves. Iris can handle a gun just fine and she's not afraid to use it." Charlie remarked as he looked over at Iris who was cleaning up the dishes.

Charlie added more wood to the fire and everyone moved in closer for the warmth. The evening was cooling down the group became tired from the day's travel.

They said their goodbyes for the night and returned to the truck. Enoch arranged the canvas to cover them as everyone bedded down for the night. The bed of the truck was hard, but when you're full and tired you don't notice such small details.

Several more vehicles arrived as the hours passed by while they slept.

CHAPTER 15

Morning arrived with the sound of someone tapping on the wood railing. It went on and on until Enoch raised up and looked around to see what the sound was. There standing at the back of the truck were several soldiers. They were dressed in battle gear and looked like they had been involved in conflict.

"We're just here to tell you that the road is open and clear to travel across. We don't know what's on the other side of those mountains, but as far as this side you shouldn't have any problems." The soldier stated, then turned and got into his vehicle and drove over to the other campsites.

Enoch looked out into the distance to a string of military vehicles that were lined up on the road. Caleb lifted from under the canvas.

"What's going on?

"They said the road is clear ahead, so we can continue on." Enoch stated as he climbed down from the back of the truck, stretched and saw the Mexican family's vehicle moving across the area to the main road.

The old pickup truck was as old as the truck they were driving and had a rusted camper on the back which stuck out several feet from behind their truck. It smoked as it moved along onto the main road passing the military vehicles and headed toward the mountain range.

"That truck sound as bad as ours. I wonder how far their going? Enoch stated.

"Well, we better get going. Let me wake everyone so we can move along." Caleb replied.

As they were preparing to leave, the RV pulled up from behind. They were all packed and had all their items covered and tied down on the top rack.

"You guys ready to go? He asked.

"We will be in a few minutes." Enoch replied.

"We'll see you on the road." He shouted out then directed the RV toward the main highway.

It took several minutes to get everything in order. But they were finally underway. Up ahead they could see the back of the RV as they traveled along the highway. Along the way they could see more memories of what used to be of the old world. More building stood vacant and others were turned into rubble. They passed through a deserted small town which appeared to be uninhabited. Through the streets was the wreckage of old vehicles turned on their sides, stripped of any usable parts. Junk of all kinds laid alongside the buildings. Old slot machines stretched across some of the streets. Enoch kept his rifle near his side but there was no movement from inside or outside the ruins.

As they followed behind the RV, they left the city and were coming closer to the lower mountain range. Up ahead they could see some smoke just off to the side of the highway. As they came closer they could see the Mexican pickup sitting alongside the road, black smoke bellowing from its engine. The RV pulled over to the side of the road.

Caleb pulled the truck behind the RV. The Mexican family was standing outside the camper.

"Well that looks like the end of the road for that truck." Charlie stated as he and Caleb walked over to the family.

"Look, why don't you gather your stuff and come with us. We have enough room." Charlie asked.

"Mario looked at his wife who was carrying a small child and nodded. It took some time for them to agree on what they needed to take. But Enoch seemed to be able to communicate with the husband as they moved items from one vehicle to another. After some time, the RV and the truck were back on the road. Caleb had stored some of the bigger items in the back and the family of three traveled in the RV.

The road ahead was clear and more vehicles were moving about. From the distance, they could see the outline of a city. Its tall buildings seemed to be more intact than others they had seen during their journey west. As they approached the cross roads a large truck was pulling wreckage away from the highway. Men moved about securing lines, cables and placing debris into another truck.

"It looks like their trying to clean the place up? Enoch shouted from the back as he and Robert stood up holding on to the wooden rails as the truck moved along.

Just off the side of the highway another tent city appeared. Much smaller in size than the last they saw. The RV pulled off the highway and stopped at the entrance. Several military soldiers stood by the entrance and approached the RV. Caleb pulled behind the RV and stopped. Like before they were questioned and their vehicle was inspected by the soldiers. Once cleared, they drove along the entrance until they reached the parking area. They were waved in and directed to an area to park. The RV parked next to an old bus that had been converted.

"The soldier said we could camp here for the rest of the day and night." Charlie stated as he helped Iris and the others out of the RV. He looked down at the ground.

"We're parked on pavement." He stated. "You know, I think this is an old air strip. Look how long it is."

"We can place the canvas across the top of both vehicles. That will give us some cover for the night." Caleb stated as he stood out looking at the tent city. "It's not as big as the last one we were at. Does anyone want to check it out?

"I want to go." Mo stated.

"Me too, I want to go." Robert replied.

"Does that family want to go with us? He asked.

"No, I think they're still a little skeptical about everything still. Iris and I will stay here with them while you're gone. We need to get things set up. They said we could have a small fire for cooking so if you're hungry don't be gone too long."

Caleb and the others walked toward the tent city. They were directed by some soldiers patrolling the area to stay in the designated areas. They followed the signs which took them to the main street where other people were gathered. Once they reached the main street several men in white coats approached them.

"Have you been checked out at the medical tent? The one man asked.

"At the last place we were at we were given shots and examined. Caleb stated as he showed him the ID card that was still around his neck.

The two men examined the cards of each person and wrote their names down on a clipboard and waved them on.

"I'm glad we kept the ID's on us. I wouldn't want to have to go through all of that again." Enoch stated.

The tent city was much smaller and had fewer businesses. There were several clothing tents and as many places to eat. Each were filled.

"I don't think the food here is any different than the last place we were at." Enoch stated. "What's that over there?

They walked to an open tent where several people where handing out boxes to other people. The boxes had something written on the side but Enoch could read it from where he was at.

"What's that say? He asked.

"I think it say, USA Food Supply." Mo stated as they moved closer.

The line was short and it didn't take long before they were standing in front of several people that appeared to be in charge.

"Do you need some supplies? The man asked as he lifted a box and started to hand it to Caleb.

"What is it? He asked.

"It's the necessary items that you need, toiletries, personal health items. Toothpaste, combs, soap, you know, the everyday stuff that you need. He takes a box." As he handed Caleb a box.

Each person took a box and carried it with them as they moved on along the street. Several other tents provided additional items and before long each person was carrying several boxes.

"This is getting a little awkward," Enoch stated. "Maybe we better get back to the camp."

"I think we just ran out of street anyway, so let's get back. Caleb stated. "Where's Mo? As they all looked around.

"She's over there at that tent talking to that lady." Robert stated.

Caleb shouted to Mo and the group began to walk back through the crowd to their camp site. Evening was approaching and the night air was cooling as it does every night when you don't have the sunlight to warm the air. The street was beginning to thin out as others began to return to their place of residence for the night. Some wondered into the sleeping tents while others walked the distance to their vehicles. The smell in the air was heavy with wood burning fires.

"Who was that you were talking to? Enoch asked Mo. "Not that it's any of my business. You usually don't talk to anyone."

"That was a trade tent where they teach you to become a nurse, nurse's aide, stuff like that. The training is free and then they give you a job after the training. She gave me some material to read."

"I guess with what's gone on in the World, nursing is a good profession to be in." Caleb stated.

They reached the camp site where Charles, Iris and the Mexican family had prepared the camp for the night.

"We need to know who these people are, what's their names," Enoch asked as he placed all the boxes down.

"This is Mario and his wife Ruth, and the babies name is Joseph. From what we could understand they were traveling to some place in Central California. I think he was saying they had family there. At least he hopes there still there." Iris stated.

Robert walked up to Mario and handed him several of the boxes he was given. Mario thanked him and showed Ruth the items that were in the box. Ruth smiled and nodded and reached out and touched Roberts hand in appreciation. Many of the necessities they didn't have.

"That was a good thing you did young man," Iris stated as she smiled at Robert.

"I'm sure they need them more than me. I still have some from the last place we stopped at." He stated.

They ate and sat around the fire. They still had most of the supplies they had gathered. Mario's wife prepared some beans while Iris had cut up some vegetables and was boiling them in the large kettle. Caleb handed out some rations boxes.

"What is this stuff? Charlie asked. "It's tough and you have to chew it a lot."

"Don't even asked," Enoch replied. "No one seems to know what it is. But you can chew on it for several days."

They stayed under the canvas for the night while Charlie and his wife stayed in the RV. Ruth, and the baby shared a place in the RV while Mario stay outside under the canvas.

The night passed by as the others began dosing off to sleep. Mo had prepared a place between Robert and Caleb.

"I think I've made a decision." Mo stated to Caleb.

"What kind of decision did you make? He asked.

"You know the women I was talking to when we were in the city getting ready to leave?

"Yeah, I remember seeing you talking to some women." He replied. "Why?

"Well, she told me that the Government is training people in the medical field and that I could become a medical aid. And I would get paid for it along with a bunch of benefits."

"Like what kind of benefits? He asked

"They would provide housing for me and placement after the training. I've never had a real job before." She stated.

"That sounds like a good thing." Caleb replied. "It sound like you're making a big decision that will affect your life." That a good thing. We all have had to make decisions like that in our lives."

"I know. So, I have decided to stay here. I wanted you guys to know." She remarked. "When you leave in the morning I'm going back and enroll. She told me I could do it first thing in the morning and to bring my things."

"Well, I think you'll do okay Mo." He replied. "If it doesn't work out you know where we are."

The sounds in the distance echoed throughout the night air. The fire had worn itself out and was smoldering. Each person was covered up with several blankets. Not a movement, not a sound by anyone.

CHAPTER 16

Caleb was busy loading the truck while Enoch was folding the canvas. He placed the canvas over the supplies in the back of the truck and tied the corners down to secure it. Caleb had taught Robert how to check the trucks fuel tanks and how to fill them. Andy had found a way to get two filled fuel drums in the back of the truck before they started which allowed them to refuel whenever necessary.

Everyone was ready and the vehicles were loaded. They drove through the entrance and reached the main road. Other vehicles were traveling in the same direction and more were headed in the opposite way.

"Where's Mo? Robert asked. "I don't see her. I thought she was up front with Caleb or in the RV."

"No, she decided to stay. I think she said she was going to get some training as a medical aid." Enoch replied. "It's just the three of us now."

They reached the mountain range and began the slowly climb up the mountain terrain stopping from time to time to allow the vehicles motors to cool. The truck strained climbing up some of the grades and came down like a bullet. It was all Caleb could do to slow it down without burning out the brakes. The lower gears provided some help, but the weight of the truck and everything that was loaded into the back made it heavy. The RV was just behind them. It too was struggling as it moved through the ups and downs of the mountains.

After several hours, they reached the top of the last mountain range and saw the valley below. Like other areas they had driven through, it too had its barren areas. Rows and rows of trees remained as a reminder of the days of the great fruit harvests. Soil that was rich for crops stood barren and dry. When they reached the base of the mountain the road made many turns. Several other vehicles could be seen traveling in their direction passing by then faded away in the distance.

Caleb pulled the truck over to an open area to allow the trucks motor to cool. The rusted relic had done its job and at times had gone be on what most thought it would be able to do. The RV pulled in behind them and parked.

Everyone got out and stretched their legs. Robert checked their fuel status of the truck and then climbed into the back of the truck and took the hose that he used to transfer fuel from the fuel drum to the gas tank. It took him several minutes to complete the fueling. It was a responsibility that was given to him and one he took seriously.

"Charlie, you need some gas? Caleb asked.

"My one tank is empty. I'm running off the other tank right now." Charlie replied. "If you can spare some that would be good."

Caleb shouted to Robert to provide Charlie with some fuel. Charlie went back to the RV and moved it closer to the truck to allow the hose to reach the RV's tank.

"You know it's not any of my business, but aren't we short one person? He asked.

"Mo decided to stay. She was offered the chance to be trained as a medical aid and decided to take advantage of the offer. I think it was the first real chance she has ever had to do something for herself." Caleb explained as they gathered near the back of the RV.

"What ever happened to the man the used to drive the truck?

"Andy? He passed away in his sleep. I never found out what he died from, probably natural causes I guess. They took him away so quickly, I never got any information. There is no funeral you know. They want to protect others from diseases so when you pass away like that they remove you and do whatever it is they do with the body to protect everyone." Caleb stated. "He was a good man."

"I guess that's best for everyone." Charlie replied.

"Are we ready to go? Caleb shouted to the others.

The RV pulled out in front with the truck followed behind it. They reached an intersection several miles down the highway and the RV pulled to the side. Caleb pulled up next to the RV and leaned over to see what the matter was.

"The sign we just passed, what's left of it says that Sacramento is to the right. That's where Mario and his wife were going, so I'm going to take them that far, then we'll try to cut across to the bay area." He explained. "If I remember right you're only about 80 miles or so from the bay area in that direction."

"Okay, we'll keep going, good luck and maybe we'll meet again." Caleb stated.

The RV pulled back on to the highway and made a

right turn at the next intersection as the others watched it disappear. Caleb, Enoch, and Robert were now by themselves as they journey through several small cities. More tent cities were visible as they continued. The open land was vast but one could see that progress to restore what had been destroyed was occurring. Men were working in areas removing wreckage and repairing buildings. Military trucks passed by carrying soldiers and for the first time the sound of a jet could be heard from inside the truck. Enoch and Robert stood up in the back, hanging on to the side rails and watched as a jet flew over. It cut through the clouds with ease and the roar of its engine was overwhelming. As quickly as it appeared it disappeared into the distant clouds, its sound following behind it.

"Where are we? Enoch shouted out.

The truck slowed down then came to a stop. Several vehicles stood parked in front of him.

"What's going on? Enoch asked.

"We're at a river crossing." Caleb replied as he climbed out of the truck.

"What river crossing? Enoch asked again as the two climbed down from the back of the truck.

Two soldiers slowly made their way to them. They were in full battle gear with weapons in hand.

"Where you headed? The one asked.

"San Francisco, but I need to cross." Caleb stated.

"Where you from? He asked, as the other walked to the rear and looked into the back of the truck.

"We just came across country from the East." Caleb replied as he watched the one soldier return.

"You came this far in this beat-up truck?

"Yeah, this beat-up truck made. So, what up here? Caleb asked.

"The bridge has only one lane. So, you're going to have to wait your turn. We're only allowing one vehicle at a time to cross." The soldier stated. "You may have trouble getting into the city. The bridge is in ruins and I don't think you'll be able to cross it. They have provided some shuttles that come and go throughout the day, but you'll have to go on foot."

"Is the way clear from here? Caleb asked.

"What I know is that they cleared most of the debris from the overpasses that collapsed so you probably will be able to at least make it to the water's edge."

They waited until they were told it was there turn to cross. The truck slowly moved across the bridge as others on the other side waited their turn. As they crossed they could see the river below. Twisted metal laid below, some in the water, and others on the shoreline. The bridge was several hundred yards in length. They finally reached the other side as those waiting cheered and waved as they passed by.

"Why are they cheering? Robert asked.

"I guess we're lucky to get across." Enoch replied.

The truck sped up and as usual a cloud of exhaust and ash filled the air.

CHAPTER 17

———————◉———————

They reached the foothills and began to climb into the coastal mountains. The clouds remained gray and the air was cool. The truck groaned, rattled, and bellowed black smoke as it slowly climbed the gradual hills. Several vehicles were parked along the side of the road. There engine hoods open.

"Why don't we stop and help? Robert asked.

"This truck is on its last leg. If we stop, we may not be able to get it up this mountain range and over to the coast." Enoch replied. "Someone will come along, probably the military and help them."

The truck continued at a slow speed for each hill was a little steeper than the next. After several miles, the road leveled out. The mountains were brown from the lack of water and most of the vegetation had vanished. The highway was clear and oncoming vehicles of all kinds passed by. Several military vehicles travel in long caravans passing the truck heading in the same direction.

"I think we need to pull over and let the old gal have a break." Caleb shouted from inside the cab.

"Since when did we decide the truck is a gal? Enoch asked as he jumped down from the back.

"I don't know, just seemed like the right thing to say." Caleb replied as they walked to the back of the truck. Robert jumped to the ground. He walked around to the side of the truck.

"Where you going? Enoch asked.

"Where do you think, I got to go," He stated.

"Oh," Enoch replied as he turned to Caleb. "Well, we haven't got too far to go now. These are the coastal mountains and just on the other side should be the bay area."

"I wonder how much of a mess it will be to get through all of that." Caleb asked.

"Mostly freeway stuff I guess. If the overpasses are still standing, you know how these big cities are with all the cars, overpasses, and underpasses." Enoch stated.

"We've got enough rations for the day so we need to get as far as we can today. This old truck is just about on its last leg. I don't know how much more we can put it through." Caleb stated.

"You know, old Andy did a good job keeping this rust bucket running." Enoch stated as he turned and kicked the tires.

"Be careful, we haven't got any spare tires." Caleb stated. "Let's put some fuel in and check the water in the radiator, then get going."

Suddenly from behind they heard a honking horn. It repeated itself over and over until it came into view as it finally reached them and pulled over behind them.

"Well look at that, Charlie and Iris caught up with us. Shows you how slow we were moving." Enoch stated as he walked up to the RV as the door opened.

"Where did you guys come from? Enoch asked as he

stood by the door and watched as Charlie came out with Iris behind them.

"We didn't need to go too far. Mario and his family decided to stay in a little town called? What was it called? He asked Iris.

"I don't remember. All those tent cities look the same to me." She replied. "There was a family they knew and decided to stay with them. But we did find someone you might be interested in seeing."

"Yeah, when he heard our story he said he knew you guys and want to tag along with us. So, we brought him along. I think they were glad to get rid of him." Iris stated with a low whisper.

"I heard that," he stated as he walked to the front of the RV and stood by the door looking down at Enoch.

"Good look who's here, it's the good Reverend." Enoch stated as he turned to Caleb.

"I thought you were........." Caleb started to say until the Reverend walked down the steps and interrupted him.

"I did what I could which was not much. They weren't very receptive to me. More people worried about their stomachs and not their souls. They convinced me I was better off somewhere else. I lasted only a few hours."

"Reverend," shouted Robert. "Are you back with us?

"If you'll let me, I'd be proud as a peacock to join you in your adventure to the blue waters of the Pacific." He replied.

"We need to get going. Do you need some fuel? Caleb asked.

"The beast climbed these mountains like a goat, but yes I could use some fuel." Charlie stated.

"Robert, that's your area. Handle that." Caleb stated.

It didn't take long before the two vehicles were again moving along the highway. They passed several cities which seemed to be one connected to the other. People were moving about and were busy working on repairing what they had lost. Many of the overpasses were destroyed but the debris was removed keeping the roads clears for travel.

Within several hours they finally reached their destination and pulled into the designated parking area. The RV pulled in alongside of the truck. An attendant walked over to them and gave each one a parking permit.

"This is good for the day. If you are going to stay longer, you need to let me know." He stated. "You need to make sure you lock your vehicle, there's been some looting going on the last several days and the military and the police have been catching some of these scumbags.

"Don't worry," Charlie stated, "I got this covered," as he reached in and brought out a double barrel shotgun.

"Where did you get that piece? Enoch stated. "I haven't seen one of those in a long time. You got shells for that?

"I had it hidden just in case there was some real trouble." Charlie stated. "I have several boxes."

"I need to find out how to get across the bay into San Francisco." Caleb stated as he looked around. "I guess I'm going to have to walk from here. Anyone who wants to go with me is welcome."

"I'll go with you." Enoch stated.

"So will I," Robert replied.

"What about you Reverend? Enoch asked.

"I don't know, let me think about it."

"Don't take too long, we're going to leave soon." Caleb stated. "Charlie, what are you and Iris going to do?

"I think we're going to stay here for a while and try to see if we can find a place for us. Iris's has some family here and we will try to make some contact with them providing there still here."

"We going to leave the truck here." Caleb stated.

"No problem, I'll take care of it. This place seems pretty secure with all these soldiers around." Charlie replied.

"You boys be careful. The City can be a dangerous place." Iris remarked.

"We will. Let's get packed up. Take what we need from the truck. We'll head out in a few." Caleb stated.

Enoch and Robert climbed back upon the truck and opened the last remaining crates of food rations. Each took several boxes and placed them into their backpacks along with several water bottles. They tied two blankets to the backpack just in case they needed them for the night. Enoch and Caleb each shoulder a rifle

"Do you need Robert to fill your tanks with the remaining fuel? Caleb asked.

"No, I can do that later."

"Charlie, if were not able to return, take what you need from the truck for yourself." Caleb stated as he walked over to Charlie and shook his hand and then gave Iris a hug. Iris turned to Enoch and Robert and gave each one a hug as well.

"Please be careful." She stated.

"I have no intentions of getting into any trouble," Enoch stated as he slipped the backpack on and secured it.

"Let's get started." Caleb said he they started to move out from the parking area.

"Hey wait for me." The Reverend shouted from behind.

They looked back to see the Reverend struggling to get his backpack on his back. It was twisted and caught on the coat he had on. Robert walked over and helped him adjust the straps and secured it.

"You made up your mind fast Reverend." Enoch stated as they watched him join up with them and walk past them.

"Let's go." He replied as he started to walk away.

"Reverend this way." Enoch stated as he pointed in the direction of the ocean.

The Reverend quickly stopped and turned around and followed behind them as they made their way through the maze of vehicles and people that were parked. Robert looked back and waved to Charlie and Iris who waved back.

From the parking structure, they stopped at the information building and asked for directions and any information that was available on entrance to the City. Several soldiers and one attendant sat behind the window. The attendant pulled out a map and instructed them on the route they should take just to get to the water edge. He then handed each of them a transit pass for the crossing the bay.

"You need to be careful. There has been some looting going on in several places along the way. I see you have weapons on you. Be careful who you shoot. There is a group of police vehicles that patrol those areas frequently. They sometime shoot first and ask questions later, if you get my meaning." The one soldier stated.

They took the map and headed in the direction that was indicated. They followed the street walking past the buildings that remained standing. Many had their windows missing and nothing remained inside. Workers were busy moving items around, loading them onto trucks while others worked inside the building.

As they reached several intersections where a jeep with several soldiers sat watching who passed by and all the activities that was going on. The soldier in the back carried an automatic weapon and appeared to be ready should any trouble start. They crossed several other intersections passing parked jeeps and continued until they reached the water front. A large sign directed them to a station with a sign in red letters, "Shuttle Service." They stood in line for some time until it was there turn at the window.

"We want to get across the bay into San Francisco." Caleb instructed the man at the window.

"So does everyone else here. You got a pass? He asked.

"Yes, we all have one." Caleb replied showing his.

"That will make it easier for you, most of these people have no passes." The attendant replied.

"How do they get across then? Enoch asked.

"They have to wait for open seats." He replied. "They'll get across, it just might take a while for it to happen. Okay, take your pass to the man standing over by the gate. Show it to him and stay close by. The next shuttle crossing will be in about fifteen minutes."

They walked over to the man at the gate and showed him the passes and were directed to wait close by. Several soldiers stood guard near the gate and many more about patrolling the area where the people were gathered. In the distance, they could hear a large craft moving in the water. The sound got loader until they saw a large water craft slowly move into position. Once it was stopped and secured, a man jumped across and walked to the gate.

"Okay, we're ready for the next load of people." He stated as they unlocked the gate and opened it to allow those with passes to move through on to the water craft. A large crowd of people, men, women and children found seats as it filled up quickly.

"Let me have ten un-ticketed people. The attendant called out names of those who had been waiting for some time for open seats. The soldiers made sure they moved through the crowd freely until they reached the gate and then boarded the craft.

Caleb, Enoch, Robert, and the Reverend moved to the back of the boat so they could view the sites as the craft moved across the water. It was a large boat. A shuttle of some kind that had been modified to carry lots of people. It was enclosed with seats inside, except for the back which remained open. The back had been modified as well with several rows of seats.

"Maybe we should have sat inside." The Reverent stated. "We might get wet here sitting in the back."

"A little sea water isn't going to hurt you." Enoch stated.

The sound of the engines could be heard as black smoke filled the air as the craft began to move away from the dock. They could hear the water churning from the propellers as it began its journey across the water to the dock of the bay. They stared at the sites as they moved, looking back from where they left and all along the pier area. Ships of all sizes stood motionless along the dock. In the distance, they could see ships moving across the water. There black smoke filling the air. A naval ship moved slowly through the water traveling out to sea. Its stacks bellowing clouds of smoke leaving a trailing wake in the sea water. As it passed by, many people waved and shouted as the water craft cut through the wake of the water. The Naval ship sounded its horn several times acknowledging those waving. Sailors on the deck waved back.

"That's a big ship." Enoch stated as he watched it pass by.

CHAPTER 18

The shuttle slowed down as it reached the landing. It maneuvered itself alongside the dock until it was in position to allow its riders off. A gated area was crowded with those who were wanting to travel out of the City as soldiers stood at the departure area keeping order.

The gate opened and those on board began to follow the directions through the gated area into the City streets. Caleb waited for the others to catch up with him as the crowd was thick and it was difficult to move freely.

They walked along the City streets observing the sites along the way. Much of the City buildings were still standing. A testimony to the engineering knowledge of man. Some of the older building were destroyed and small amounts of framework stood as a reminder of how it used to be. The streets were being cleared and most of the debris had already been cleared away. Crews were working repairing streets while other crews were tearing down what was left of the older buildings.

They walked uphill for several hours and then had to stop to rest. The clouded sky made the air cool and at times they felt a mist in the air.

"The only thing missing here is some fog." Enoch stated.

"I tell you what's missing is the cable cars." The Reverend stated. "My legs are killing me walking through these uphill streets. How much further do we have?

"You see that building up ahead. The one on the left where the street poles are laying on the ground. Just on the other side of that." Caleb stated. "There should be a row of small building just behind it."

They continued until they reached the building. As they got closer Caleb became nervous and stopped.

"What's the matter? Enoch asked.

"I haven't been here in so many years." Caleb replied. "I think I'm afraid to see what's on the other side."

As they walked past the last remaining building they could see what was before them. The small house that was his childhood home, where his father had lived was leveled to the ground. The old structure was nothing more than a pile of wood and brick.

"This place didn't make it," The Reverend stated. "Are you sure this is the place?

"Yeah, this is the place," Caleb replied. "The rock fence is still standing."

"Maybe he got out? Robert stated as he walked around viewing the remains of the home.

"You men got no business being here, now move on." A voice shouted out.

They turned quickly to see an elderly man standing at the remains of the home next door.

"Go on now, move along." He shouted again.

"I'm looking for the man who lived here." Caleb asked.

"Why you want to know? He asked. "You some kind of relative?

"Actually he is," The Reverend stated. "He's the son of the man who lived here."

"The son? He replied. "The man who lived here had only one son. Let me see, what was his name? The elderly man thought for several minutes.

"We haven't all day, this is Caleb." Enoch stated. "And this used to be his father's home."

"You the boy, I remember you when you were little. Where you been anyway? You father used to talk about you all the time.

"'I've been in the East coast." Caleb replied. "Where is my father now, did he survive?

"You father, like most of us got out just in time. They took us to the shelter. This is what we're left with, nothing but a pile of wood and brick."

"You're Mr. Cambridge. I remember you now." Caleb stated as he stepped forward. You used to have a little dog. When I tried to pet it, it would nip at me all the time."

"Yeah, that was toots. He's been dead for many years now."

"So, where's my father now? Caleb asked.

"I would think he's still at the shelter. He was there when I left and came here. I live in the back. Built me a little shelter of my own." He stated.

"Which way is the shelter? Caleb asked.

"Go down to the end of the street, turn left and follow the shelter signs. You'll find it. He remarked.

Caleb and the others left and hurried up the street to the intersection and turned left. Shelter signs were posted along the way in big red letters. At the next intersection, they could see a large sign with an arrow pointing to the entrance door of the shelter. Two men stood outside. When they finally reached the door the two men stepped in front of them.

"Where you think you're going? The larger man asked.

"I'm going inside the shelter to find my father." Caleb replied.

"No you're not. Not unless you got something to pay your way in with. What you got under that coat?

"He's got the same thing I've got under my coat. Let me show you." Enoch stated as he stepped forward, opened his coat and pointed the rifle at the two men. "This is our pass to go where ever we want to go."

The two men were surprised at the sight of the rifle. They looked at one another and stepped aside. Caleb pushed them aside and opened the door.

"You want to go in with me? He asked.

"We'll stay out here and take care of business. Take Robert with you. Things could get messy." Enoch stated.

Caleb and Robert entered the shelter and stopped at the information window. Behind the glass was two attendants with large books in front of them.

"Can I help you? He asked.

"I'm looking for my father." Caleb asked.

"Okay, give me his name and let me see if he's still here. Many people have left already."

Caleb gave him all the information that he knew on his father. Name, approximate age, where he lived. The attendant continued to ask other questions which were difficult for Caleb to answer since he'd been gone for such a long time.

"Here it is, right here, Adam Cantu is in section 2B. It appears he's still here."

"Which way." He asked.

"Down that hallway and 2B is to the left. 2A will be on the right. Go down until you reach section B and he should be in there somewhere."

Caleb and Robert hurried down the hallway until they reached the sign indicating 2B. They turned left and followed it passing several housing units until they reached section B. They stopped at the doorway and looked in. The housing unit was half filled with people moving about. Beds filled the side walls in rows as the two walked down the center walkway.

"How do you know who's who here? Robert asked.

"I don't know." Caleb replied they continued walking.

A large man approached them carrying a broom and a small bucket.

"Can I help you? He asked.

"Yes, I'm looking for my father." Caleb stated. "His name is......."

"Caleb is that you? A voice could be heard from behind them.

Caleb and Robert turned quickly to see an elderly man lying in a cot just behind them. He lifted himself up from the cot and peered at the two. He was thin and pale. His white hair was thick and uncared for. His face was thin and his bony features could be seen.

"I thought that was you." He stated. "I remember your voice."

Caleb quickly stepped to the cot. Father is that you? He asked as he got down on his knees next to the cot. He took his father's hand in his and held it tight. It was thin and cool to the touch.

"It's what left of me," he stated. "I knew you would come. Who is the boy?

"This is Robert, he's been with me all the way here. He helped me get out of the city and he's traveled with us to help find you." Caleb stated.

"There's more of you? He asked.

"There's two more, there outside, out front. We had a little trouble getting in here. Two men wanted what they couldn't have. Enoch and the Reverend are outside trying to make honest men of them." Robert stated.

"How long have you been in here? Caleb asked.

"When things started to get bad, the military sent truck around picking up people and bringing them to the shelter. I've been here ever since, I guess maybe 4 years."

"I went to the house looking for you." Caleb replied.

"What's it look like? He asked.

"It's just a pile of brick and wood right now. Your neighbor was there. He built himself a shack in the back of his house to live in. He says he going to rebuild it." Caleb stated.

"That might take him some time." His father stated as he laid back down on the cot.

"No, that's what where going to do. Rebuild the house." Caleb stated as he looked at Robert.

"Rebuild the house? Robert asked.

"That's right, rebuild the house." He replied. "Do you remember the camping we used to do and that giant canvas tent you made for us to stay in? Caleb asked

"I think I do, yeah it was stored in the back of the garage." His father replied.

"You still got? He asked.

"Yeah, it was in the back somewhere. Is the garage still standing? He asked.

"Part of it is, besides whether it is or is not we can dig it out and there's plenty of room in the back of the house to put it up." Caleb stated. "And I got some guys who might be able to help me."

Caleb spent the rest of the hour with his father. They talked until he became tired. They agreed upon a plan and the two left with the understanding that they would be back in the morning to talk more about what they were about to undertake.

Caleb and Robert exited the shelter to the street. Enoch and the Reverend were leaning against the building as Caleb and Robert closed the door to the shelter.

"Okay, we found him, we talked with him and we made a plan with him." Caleb stated. "Why are those two men tied to that pole?

"It's funny you asked that," The Reverend stated. The soldiers who came by a few minutes ago asked the same thing."

"What happened? Robert asked.

"They weren't very cooperative when you left. And the one told Enoch something that made him mad, so, and you know how Enoch is, he tied them to the pole, took their shoes and threw them unto the roof of that building over there somewhere." The Reverend explained.

They looked at Enoch who just smiled. "How's your father? He asked.

"Good. He's weak, but he's good." Caleb replied. "But I need to talk to you guys about something. I know you have travel with me since we left the East and we've gone through a lot together. And if you say no, that's okay, I'll understand. I need help rebuilding my father's house. He can't stay in the shelter for ever and I think we can make a place that will provide all of us a living space." Caleb explained.

"Build a house? How big a house? Enoch asked.

"Big enough for a place for him and a place for each of you as well. He has the tools in the garage and a large tent we can use to live in while we build it."

"I don't mind doing that, I used to be a carpenter when I was a young man." The Reverend stated.

"Tell you what, if we build this house and a place for each of us can we also include a BBQ in the back yard? I really miss having a BBQ." Enoch asked

"You can build a boat in the back if you want." Caleb replied.

"Good for me," Enoch stated.

"I'm in." Robert stated with a confident smile on his face.

"Can I have a bath tube? The Reverend asked.

"Reverend, you can have a bath tub and a pond in the back to float around in and anything else you want."

"I'm in." The Reverend stated.

"Let's get going, we have a lot to do." Caleb replied.

"I need to find a church." The Reverend stated.

"What's up? Enoch asked

"We'll need a little help, and I know where to get it." The Reverend said as he pointed upward.

121

"Got you." Enoch stated as he pointed upward as well.

Robert looked upward, not understanding the meaning but figured it must be okay if Enoch was agreeing with it. He slowly raised his finger up as well as everyone watched and then laughed. They were home.

CONCLUSION

————◉————

The World was devastated by what man had created, the motives behind his decisions, and the amount of power he held in his hand. A push of a button by all involved and the destiny of the World was changed. What gain was there after it was over? The suffering, pain, and death of those who had nothing to do with its decisions is be on description, be on understanding.

But man, seems to find a way to survive and did, and in time he will eventually replace the objects that he had created and even make them better. The World needed to repair itself, by itself, and it did, and that also took time.

To place that kind of power in the hands of individuals can be dangerous. I'd rather have them stand in front of each other and throw rocks at one another. Think about it.

Is it the

THE END

Printed in the United States
By Bookmasters